Harriet opened her eyes to see James standing in a shaft of moonlight at the end of the bed.

She smiled at him drowsily for a moment, and then shot upright in shock. It was no dream. He was here, in the flesh.

'I frightened you,' said James tersely. 'I'm sorry. I didn't expect to find you here.'

She pulled the sheet up over the heart banging against her ribs. 'But you knew I was coming to La Fattoria.'

'I meant here in my room.'

'Oh.' She heaved in a shaky breath. 'I didn't know it was your room.'

James took in a deep breath. 'Go back to sleep. We'll talk in the morning.'

The door closed behind him and Harriet's heart was still thumping from the shock of finding a man in her ro~~om. O~~ ~~it~~ ~~~~ an, it was James. ~~~~ ~~~~ then snatched at he~~~~ flew open and Jam~~~~

D0893215

Catherine George was born in Wales, and early on developed a passion for reading which eventually fuelled her compulsion to write. Marriage to an engineer led to nine years in Brazil, but on his later travels the education of her son and daughter kept her in the UK. And instead of constant reading to pass her lonely evenings she began to write the first of her romantic novels. When not writing and reading she loves to cook, listen to opera, browse in antiques shops and walk the Labrador.

Recent titles by the same author:

TANGLED EMOTIONS
CITY CINDERELLA
SARAH'S SECRET
SWEET SURRENDER

THE UNEXPECTED PREGNANCY

BY
CATHERINE GEORGE

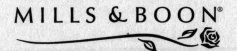

MILLS & BOON®

*First published in Great Britain 2004
Harlequin Mills & Boon Limited,
Eton House, 18-24 Paradise Road, Richmond, Surrey TW9 1SR*

© Catherine George 2004

ISBN 0 263 83774 2

*Set in Times Roman 10½ on 11½ pt.
01-0904-50937*

*Printed and bound in Spain
by Litografia Rosés, S.A., Barcelona*

CHAPTER ONE

HARRIET let herself into the still, empty house, but instead of making her usual nostalgic tour went straight to the kitchen to make a pot of the expensive coffee brought along for brain fuel. It was crunch time. She had to get to grips right away with the problem she'd taken a week's holiday leave to solve. Before she went back to London a decision had to be made about her legacy. Her grandmother had made it very clear in her will that End House and its contents were to be left to Harriet to dispose of exactly as she wished. But what she *wished*, thought Harriet fiercely, was that her grandmother were still alive, and that any minute she'd come in from the garden with a bunch of herbs in her hand, demanding help to make supper.

When the coffee-pot was empty Harriet took her bags upstairs and, because this might be the last time she ever slept here, put them in her grandmother's room for the first time instead of her own. She ran a caressing hand over the brass rails of the bed, hung up some of her things in the oak armoire, and folded the rest away in the beautiful Georgian chest. Olivia Verney had disapproved of clothes flung down on chairs. Harriet grinned as she made up the bed. A good thing her grandmother had never seen her flatmate's bedroom. Dido Parker was a good friend, and good at her job, but tidy she was not.

After supper Harriet made some phone calls to announce her arrival, watered the array of plants in the conservatory, and had just settled down to read in the last of the evening light when she heard a car stop outside. She got up to look, and dodged back in dismay when she recognised the driver.

But there was no point in hiding behind the sofa. Tim had probably told his brother she was here.

When the knock came on the door, Harriet counted to five before opening it to confront the tall figure of James Edward Devereux.

She gave him a cool smile. 'Hello. I'm afraid Tim's not here. I came on my own.'

'I know that. May I come in?'

As if she could refuse, she thought irritably, and showed him into the small, elegantly furnished sitting room.

Her visitor was silent for a moment as he looked at his surroundings. 'It's months since your grandmother died, but here in her house it seems only right to offer my condolences again, Harriet.'

'Thank you. Do sit down.'

'I liked your grandmother very much,' he said, choosing Olivia Verney's favourite chair. 'I was deeply sorry I couldn't make it to the funeral. I went down with some virus at the time.'

'I heard.' She perched on the edge of the sofa, feeling edgy. She'd known Tim's brother since she was thirteen years old, and lately she'd even run into him in London once or twice, but they'd never been alone together before. What on earth was he doing here?

'It must have been a shock when she left you so suddenly,' he said with sympathy.

Harriet nodded soberly. 'A shock for me, but great for her.'

'True.' James Devereux became suddenly businesslike. 'Right, then, Harriet, I'll get to the point. Did Mrs Verney tell you I'd approached her about selling the house to me?'

She stared at him blankly. '*This* house?'

'Yes. The others in the row already belong to Edenhurst—'

'You mean to you.'

'Yes, Harriet, to me,' he said patiently. 'I need more staff accommodation, and End House would be ideal.'

'Sorry,' she said instantly. 'It's not for sale.'

His eyes narrowed. 'Tim told me you were spending a week here to come to a decision.'

'I am.'

'So when did you arrive?'

'A couple of hours ago.'

'And the decision's already made?' His smile was mocking as he got to his feet. 'Tell me, Harriet. If someone else had made the offer would you have accepted?'

'It's nothing personal,' she said, lying through her teeth. 'I just don't want to sell End House right now.'

'But Tim said you'd had it valued.'

'On his advice, yes,' she said curtly, making a note to have strong words with Tim Devereux.

He looked at her thoughtfully. 'If I offered slightly more than the estimate, would that change your mind?'

'It most certainly would not!' Her eyes flashed. 'And Tim had no right to discuss the price with you.'

'He didn't. I asked the estate agent who sold me the other three.'

'You needn't have bothered. End House is not for sale.'

'Before I go, enlighten me, Harriet,' he said, following closely as she marched out into the hall. 'Why are you always so damned hostile towards me?'

She turned a scornful smile on him. 'It's no mystery. You make it pretty obvious lately that you disapprove of my relationship with Tim.'

'You surely realise why?'

'I've never given it a thought,' she told him, amazed that her nose failed to grow a couple of inches at the lie.

'Then think about it now,' he said crisply. 'I've had to be father, mother *and* brother to Tim since he was ten. I don't want to see him hurt.'

She bristled. 'You think *I'm* going to hurt him?'

'Yes.' His eyes held hers. 'Tim's a one-woman man, but I know that you have other men in your life. I'd say the odds on Tim getting hurt are fairly high.'

Not for the first time in their acquaintance Harriet wanted to punch James Edward Devereux on his elegant nose. Instead she opened the door wide to speed him on his way. 'Tim's perfectly happy with the fact that I have friends of both sexes.'

'In the same situation I couldn't be happy with that.'

'You and Tim are two very different people,' she said coldly.

'True. Everyone loves Tim. Goodnight, Harriet.' James Devereux glanced back as he reached his car. 'The offer will stay on the table for a while. Ring me if you change your mind.'

Harriet closed the door, rammed the bolts home and stormed to the kitchen to make a pot of coffee black and strong enough to counteract the effect James Devereux invariably had on her.

She'd met his brother Tim in the village post office when she first came to live with her grandmother in Upcote, and the two orphaned thirteen-year-olds had taken to each other on sight. Tim had raced back to End House with Harriet right away to ask Olivia Verney's permission to take her granddaughter fishing in the stream that ran through Edenhurst grounds. And afterwards he'd taken Harriet off to meet his brother, who was twelve years Tim's senior, and possessed of such striking good looks he'd seemed like a god from Olympus to the youthful Harriet.

Tim so openly worshipped his brother that for a while Harriet had found it natural to follow suit. Unlike her friends at school, who had crushes on rock stars and football players, Harriet Verney's naive form of hero-worship had centred on James Edward Devereux. Tall, self-assured, with glossy dark hair and the tawny Devereux eyes, he was the archetypal Corsair to a teenager just introduced to Byron's poetry.

During that first summer vacation with her grandmother, Harriet had come to terms with her first experience with grief. The double loss of her parents in a storm on a sailing holiday had broken her world in pieces, and it had taken all her grandmother's loving care to put it back together again. The meeting with Tim accelerated the healing process. That summer Harriet spent most of her daylight hours with him. Totally comfortable in each other's company, they ate at the kitchen table at End House with Olivia Verney, or ran free on the acres of land belonging to Edenhurst, the beautiful, but increasingly dilapidated home of the Devereux brothers.

By that time both Devereux parents had been dead for some time and life had become difficult for the heir to the estate. Crippling inheritance tax, plus school fees for Tim and wages for even the bare minimum of staff required to keep Edenhurst going had all been a huge burden for a young man only just qualified as an architect. Through Tim Harriet had learned that some of the antique furniture and the more valuable family paintings had to be sold. With the proceeds as back-up James Devereux had taken a gamble, and with a partner set up a company to convert derelict warehouses into expensive riverside apartments.

The gamble paid off, the apartments sold like hot cakes, and riding high on the success of the enterprise James Devereux eventually went on to transform Edenhurst into the first of a series of hotels with integral health spas. He married an established star in the modelling world, and the only cloud on the dynamic young entrepreneur's horizon had been his brother's flat refusal to join the company.

Tim Devereux insisted on taking a fine art degree instead, and went straight from college to work in a London gallery owned by Jeremy Blyth, an art dealer highly respected in his field. None of Tim's choices had been influenced by Harriet, but James made it plain he blamed her for all of them, even though Tim was adamant that nothing would have persuaded him to go into property developing. The new job suited him down to the ground. Jeremy Blyth was charming, witty, openly gay and knew all there was to know about the art world. The job would provide invaluable experience, also allow spare time for Tim's own painting. He shared a house with two friends from art college and he had Harriet. What else could he want in life?

'His lordship's blessing?' she'd said bluntly.

'I don't know why you're always so down on Jed.' Tim had given her a coaxing smile as he put an arm round her. 'Come on, Harry. Get if off your chest at last. You and I don't have secrets, remember. What is it with you and my brother?'

He'd kept on about it until at last, desperate to shut him up, Harriet finally told him that one Sunday afternoon she'd stopped to stroke the dog outside the open kitchen door of Edenhurst, overheard James lecturing Tim, and suffered the usual fate of eavesdroppers.

'He felt great sympathy for my situation, but thought you should see something of the lads from the village as well, instead of spending all your time with a girl—even one who looked just like a boy with such close cropped hair and a gruff little voice.' She growled at the memory, which still burned. 'I wanted to kill him with my bare hands!'

Tim had roared with laughter. 'You've changed a bit since then, tiger. The hair grew, the girl equipment arrived, and that voice of yours could earn a fortune these days on one of those sexy chat lines—ouch!' he howled as she hit him. 'And now he's shackled to the fair Madeleine surely you feel *some* sympathy for Jed.'

'Not a scrap! He's far too overbearing and sure of himself to merit any sympathy from me.'

From that day on Harriet never thought of or referred to James Edward Devereux as Jed, as he was known to family and friends. And she never told a soul that her teenage self-esteem had been dealt such a blow that summer afternoon it had taken years afterwards for her to think of herself as even passably attractive.

Harriet rang Dido early next morning to say she'd received an offer for End House. 'Tim's brother wants to add it to the Edenhurst estate, but I just can't face giving the house up yet, so I turned him down.'

'Good God, are you mad?' said Dido, shocked. 'I know your grandma left money to keep the place going for six months, but from now on you'll have to pay running costs yourself.'

'I know all that. But it's been my home for the past ten years, remember. I just can't bear to part with it yet. In fact,' added Harriet, bracing herself, 'I thought I might even live here myself for a bit, Dido.'

There was a pause. 'You work in London,' Dido reminded her, sounding close to tears.

'I could look round for something in this area instead— Cheltenham, maybe.'

'You really want to desert me?'

Harriet felt a guilty pang. 'You earn serious money these days. Couldn't you manage the mortgage on your own?'

'I don't care about the beastly mortgage. I just want you here with me. Besides, what about Tim?'

'We can see each other at weekends.'

'I think you're making a huge mistake, Harriet. Please don't make any snap decisions.'

Harriet spent some time reassuring her friend, then walked to the village shops to buy a newspaper, stopped to chat with a couple of people she knew, and, because it was such a beautiful day, took the longer route back along the small tributary that formed the boundary to Edenhurst. She paused as she reached the stepping stones she'd hopped across so often with Tim in the past, and on impulse took off her sandals to see how far she could get. Halfway across she discovered that the water was faster and deeper than she remembered. She turned to retrace her steps, wobbled precariously as she hung on to her sandals, but lost her newspaper to the current when she spotted James Devereux in the shade of the willow hanging over the far bank.

'Want some help?' he asked, grinning broadly.

'No,' she said through her teeth.

To her annoyance he kicked off his shoes and strolled across the stones towards her, sure-footed as a panther. 'Give me your hand,' he ordered.

Harriet hesitated, almost lost her balance, and James grabbed her hand and hauled her across the stream straight up the bank into Edenhurst territory.

'Now I've saved you from a ducking I claim a reward,' he said, collecting his shoes. 'Have lunch with me, Harriet. No wedding or conference this weekend. It's fairly peaceful here for once.'

Harriet eyed him in astonishment as she thrust damp feet into her sandals. 'If this is a ploy to win me over about End House it won't work.'

'Certainly not. I just think it's time you and I tried to get along better, for Tim's sake.' His lips twitched. 'Besides, when I'm bent on persuasion—of any kind—I tend towards champagne and caviare.'

'I detest caviare.'

'I'll make a note of that.' He smiled persuasively. 'But right now a humble sandwich is the only thing involved. So what do you say?'

She looked at him for a moment, then gave a reluctant nod. 'All right.'

His lips twitching at her lack of enthusiasm, James rang the house to order a picnic lunch in the folly. 'I remember the days when you ran wild round here, Harriet,' he commented as they began climbing the steep, winding path. He glanced at her fleetingly. 'You've changed out of all recognition since then. The clothes are not much different, I suppose, but the resemblance ends there, full stop. At one time it was hard to tell you from Tim, whereas now—'

'Whereas now,' she cut back at him, 'my hair's long and you can tell exactly what sex I am. But I'm stuck with the voice.'

He stopped dead at a stile blocking the path, comprehension dawning in his eyes. 'Is this something *I* said?'

'I once overheard you trying to persuade Tim to spend less time with me and more with the village boys.' Harriet smiled sweetly. 'If you were trying to turn him off me it didn't work.'

'Quite the reverse! Tim's been crazy about you since he was fourteen years old.'

'Thirteen,' corrected Harriet.

'Unlucky for some,' James said lightly, and startled her considerably by picking her up to deposit her on the other side of the stile.

By the time they reached the mock-Grecian temple where she'd once played endless games with Tim, their lunch was waiting on the stone bench girdling the interior. The tray held fresh fruit, a covered silver dish of sandwiches and an opened bottle of red wine.

James poured a glass for Harriet, and sat down beside her on the bench to remove the cover from the platter. 'Definitely no caviare,' he assured her.

'Quite a choice just the same,' she said, impressed. 'Is

that how things work for you all the time, James? You just wave a wand and—what have I said?'

'You actually allowed my given name to pass your lips!' He raised his glass in mocking toast. 'To truce, Harriet, long may it last. Now, what would madam like? Ham, smoked salmon, and, yes, I do believe there's good old cheese as well.'

'Very good old cheese,' she said, tasting it.

Harriet took a long, affectionate look at the house while they ate in surprisingly comfortable silence for a minute or two. Edenhurst's limestone architecture was typical of the area, with dips built into the steeply pitched roof to keep the tiles in place, and small-paned casement windows protected by stone mullions and drip-courses. But Harriet felt a sudden, sharp stab of nostalgia. Now it was restored and renovated as a luxury hotel, with park-perfect gardens, Edenhurst wore an air of affluence very different from the shabby charm of the past.

'What are you thinking?' said James.

'That in some ways I preferred the house the way it was when I first came here.'

He smiled wryly. 'A romantic viewpoint! To me it was an endless juggle of resources in those days, to decide which repair to do next.'

'Tim told me that.' Harriet cast a glance at him as she took another sandwich. 'My grandmother was deeply impressed by the way you tackled the problem.'

'So she told me. She was a very special lady.' His mouth turned down. 'It went against the grain to part with any family possessions, but I had no choice. Then I had a stroke of luck when a college friend put some capital in with mine to found the company.' He shook his head reminiscently. 'God, how we worked—twenty hours a day in the beginning.'

'It certainly paid off. The rest is history.' Harriet smiled crookedly. 'You know, it amazes me that this is happening.'

'You and me, alone, breaking bread together?'

'Exactly.'

His eyes glinted as he refilled her glass. 'Even though I'm the wicked squire trying to evict you from your home?'

'Trying to tempt me out of it with an inflated offer!'

'Not inflated at all. End House possesses a larger garden than its neighbours, remember, plus a conservatory.'

Harriet sighed. 'My friend thinks I'm mad to refuse such a good offer, but it's hard to part with the house. It's been my home for a long time. Besides, selling it is too much like a final break from my grandmother—who was a practical soul, and would laugh me out of court for being so sentimental.'

'I see your point.' James looked at her searchingly. 'But if selling is out of the question are you thinking of letting it instead?'

'I did consider that, but a solicitor friend of mine pointed out some of the drawbacks of being a landlord.' She sighed. 'If I thought I could get work in the area I'd live at End House myself.'

'You might find life in Upcote a little quiet after London, so think it over very carefully before you make a decision,' he advised.

'I came down here to do just that. But it means a week less for my holiday in Italy with Tim later on,' added Harriet with regret.

'Tim told me he's persuaded you to go to La Fattoria at last.' James frowned. 'Doesn't he mind that you're cutting the holiday short?'

'Only my part of it.' Harriet shrugged. 'Tim's going on ahead for the first week. He doesn't mind.'

'Because where Tim's concerned you can do no wrong.' She put her glass down on the tray with a click. 'You just don't understand my relationship with Tim. We don't live in each other's pockets. If he wants to do something independently I'm perfectly happy with that, and the reverse also applies.'

James shook his head. 'I'd be anything but happy in the same circumstances.'

'Really?' said Harriet sweetly. 'If that was your attitude with Madeleine no wonder she took off.'

He got up, his handsome face suddenly blank as he stacked the remains of their lunch on the tray. 'You know nothing about my marriage, young lady.'

'No, indeed—I beg your pardon.' Harriet jumped to her feet, her face hot. 'I'd better go.'

'Why? What's so pressing at End House that you can't stay for coffee?' He smiled a little, his eyes warming again. 'You know how easy it is to get service round here. I just wave my wand.'

Harriet shook her head. 'No, thanks.'

'Then I'll walk you home.'

'Unnecessary.'

James raised an eyebrow. 'Truce over already?'

'Of course not. It's only practical to keep on civil terms.' She gave him a direct look. 'If only for Tim's sake.'

'Point taken. By the way,' he added, 'Tim's been throwing out hints about a wedding.'

'It's far too soon to talk about that.'

James shrugged. 'He'll tell me soon enough when you name the day. He couldn't keep a secret to save his life. He'll be pleased that we had lunch together,' he added.

'I'm sure he will.' She smiled politely. 'Thank you. It was delicious.'

'My pleasure. I take a walk round the grounds every morning when I'm here, but I've never been lucky enough to meet a fair maiden in need of rescue before.'

'At one time I could hop across those stones with no

trouble at all.' She pulled a face. 'My sense of balance was better when I was thirteen.'

He smiled ruefully. 'I apologise for trying to turn Tim off you all those years ago, Harriet. I just wanted to give him some back-up with the village lads when you weren't around. Without you he was always like a lost soul.' The familiar tawny eyes, so like and yet so unlike Tim's, held hers. 'Am I forgiven?'

'Of course,' she said lightly. 'Goodbye.'

Harriet chose the more formal route home via the main gates in preference to getting her feet wet again, called in at the village stores to buy another newspaper, and walked back to End House deep in thought. The unexpected picnic had by no means been an ordeal. For most of the time the atmosphere over lunch had been relatively amicable. And Tim would be delighted that she'd thawed even a little towards his brother. Not that she was likely to see more of James while she was here. She knew from Tim that to keep his staff on their toes James made brief unheralded visits to all his properties and at Edenhurst the stable block had been converted into private quarters for the Devereux brothers. But James was the only one to use them. Tim had taken to metropolitan life like a duck to water and kept well away from Edenhurst now it was a hotel.

The two brothers, thought Harriet, could hardly be less alike. Tim was slight and fair, with boyish good looks and a natural charm that made women yearn to mother him. Her lips curved in a cynical smile. Of all the emotions James Devereux stirred up in the opposite sex, maternal leanings probably never made the list.

CHAPTER TWO

HARRIET found a note pushed through the door when she got back to End House.

'Harriet, if you're here for the week will you want me on Monday as usual? Regards, Stacy.'

Harriet was more than capable of looking after one small house for a week, especially on her own, without the mayhem Dido created in their London flat. But because Stacy Dyer was a single parent who needed the money Harriet rang to ask her to come in as usual.

After spending the rest of the day in the sunshine in the back garden Harriet had an early night, and next morning, in contrast to the hectic rush of London routine, she read in bed for a while before getting up to enjoy a leisurely bath. But as she lingered over breakfast later she felt a touch of panic. What was she going to do for the rest of the day, let alone the rest of the week? After all her fine talk about living here it was a bit of a blow to find she'd had enough of it already. Living alone here on a permanent basis was very different from odd weekends away from London.

Harriet faced the truth as she washed her breakfast dishes. Her knee-jerk reaction to James' offer had been ill-advised. She might never get another as generous. And, painful though it was to part with End House, she needed the money as security now she was alone in the world. She would stay until the weekend to save face, and then sell End House to James Devereux.

Harriet found an old cagoule in the closet, put money in the pocket and went off with an umbrella to the village stores to buy a Sunday paper. By the time she got back the sun was out, and she could hear Livvie's voice reminding her that a garden needed weeding whether she was selling the house or not. Armed with fork and trowel, and a large waste bag for the weeds, Harriet prepared to do battle. End House gave directly onto the street in front, but owned a sizeable garden at the back, with apple trees and flowering shrubs. The laurel hedges were still reasonably neat, courtesy of the man who'd always helped her grandmother, but now Harriet could no longer afford to keep him the lawn needed mowing, and the herbaceous borders were fast getting out of hand.

Harriet got to work, but after only half an hour or so she was sweating and grubby, her neck ached, and only a discouragingly small portion of border was weed-free. She went indoors, gulped down a glass of water, and then set to it once more, determined to clear at least as much ground again before she took another breather. One thing was certain, she found, panting as she tugged and pulled, she'd hit on a sure way to kill time. Gardening looked a lot easier on television. She got to her feet at last to stretch her aching back, and groaned silently in frustration when she saw James Devereux strolling along the side path towards her.

'Hello, Harriet.'

'Hi. You're still here, then.' Oh, well done, Harriet. Top marks.

'Interviews this week,' he said briefly. 'Am I interrupting?'

'No, I've just finished. Did you want something?'

He looked at her levelly. 'I just called in to say hello.'

Or to put pressure on her about the sale, more likely. Reminding herself that this was a good thing now she'd made her decision she smiled brightly. 'Come inside. I'll just dispose of this stuff first.' Harriet put her gardening tools away and led her visitor into the kitchen. 'Would you like a drink, or some tea?'

'Tea would be good.'

Harriet washed her hands and filled the kettle, wishing that her shorts were longer and less encrusted with mud and sweat. 'Do sit down,' she told him as she hunted out teapot and cups.

James took one of the rush-seated chairs at the table, watching her objectively as she laid a tray and put tea bags in the pot. 'You were the same height at thirteen. I remember those long legs of yours.'

She glanced up in astonishment as she filled the teapot and splashed boiling water on her wrist in the process.

James leapt from his chair at her anguished gasp. 'Did you scald yourself?' he demanded, seizing her hand.

'Not much,' she said faintly. 'It's just a drop or two.'

James turned the cold tap on in the sink and held her wrist under the water. 'You're trembling,' he said gently, and put his arm round her. 'Shock, probably.'

If so he was making it a whole lot worse. She could feel the heat of his body through the thin shirt, a faint aura of citrus and spice mingled with the scent of warm male skin—and he's Tim's *brother*, she reminded herself in horror, limp with relief when James released her and turned off the tap.

'That's better. Sit down, Harriet.' He put the lid on the pot, poured tea, passed a cup to her, and sat down at the table. 'Why didn't Tim come down with you for the weekend before going off to Paris?'

'I needed time on my own to make my mind up about the house,' she told him gruffly, utterly floored by the discovery that James Devereux was a man she was attracted to. At least, her body was. Her brain flatly refused to believe it.

James eyed her downcast face thoughtfully. 'If you

change your mind and sell the house to me, Harriet, you could buy a flat of your own. Tim tells me you're tired of sharing with your friend.'

Tim, she thought irritably, should keep his big mouth shut. 'It's a tempting prospect,' she agreed.

James leaned forward. 'But frankly it astonishes me that you and Tim haven't set up house together long before this. Are you waiting to get married first?'

Harriet paused for a heartbeat, and then raised dark, demure eyes to his. 'I'm old-fashioned that way.'

James sat back again, frowning. 'And how does Tim feel about that?'

'He agrees with me.'

'This time you really do amaze me! No wonder he's talking about a wedding soon.'

She looked him in the eye. 'Frankly I'm surprised you're such a keen advocate of marriage.'

'Don't be put off by my example.' His face shadowed. 'You and Tim are soul mates. Madeleine and I were not. But I apologise for snapping at you on the subject yesterday, Harriet. Tim would create hell if he knew I'd upset you in any way.'

'You didn't,' she assured him. 'Have some more tea.'

James shook his head and got up. 'I must go. How is your hand now?'

'Fine.'

'Good. Be more careful in future.'

And to Harriet's surprise he took himself off, leaving her mystified as to why he'd come to see her again. Surely not just to apologise for a remark he'd had every right to make! He'd made no further attempt to persuade her into selling, and if his aim was to sound her out about wedding plans he was out of luck. She smoothed her reddened wrist, reliving her physical reaction to James Devereux's touch. At the mere thought of it a shiver ran through her entire body, right down to her toes, but she shook it off angrily. He was Tim's brother, for heaven's sake.

During the evening Tim rang up for a chat before his departure for Paris on business, astonished when she told him she'd seen his brother on three occasions so far, one of which had entailed a picnic lunch in the Edenhurst folly.

'Which reminds me,' she said, militant because she felt guilty for a sin not even committed, 'in future don't discuss my personal affairs with all and sundry.'

'I do nothing of the kind,' he said indignantly. 'But if you mean End House, Jed asked about it so I told him.'

'He wants it as staff accommodation for Edenhurst.'

'Pretty urgently if he's popping in on you all the time.'

'Thanks a lot!'

'You know what I mean, Harry.'

'I do know. By the way, *dearest*, he asked why you and I aren't living together right now.'

He whistled. 'And what did you say to to that?'

'I made it clear I disapprove of cohabiting before marriage,' she said primly.

'You're kidding me!' Tim gave the uproarious laugh that always had Harriet joining in. 'I do love you, Harry.'

'I love you, too. Enjoy yourself.'

Harriet put down the phone, unsurprised that Tim had no idea how miserable she felt under all the banter. Their relationship was unique and very special to them both, but secretly it was very different from the one they made it out to be. Usually she had no problem with this, but today she had experienced James Devereux's touch for the first time. And found it was a dangerously inflammable sensation never experienced before with any man, including Tim. Especially Tim. Yet in the circumstances she had to try and forget it had ever happened. If she could.

* * *

Stacy Dyer arrived at nine on the dot the following morning, complete with black eye and a baby boy fast asleep in a pushchair.

'I had to bring Robert with me today,' she said anxiously. 'Do you mind?'

'Of course I don't mind!' Harriet smiled down at the sleeping child. 'He's gorgeous, Stacy. Have some coffee before you start. How did you get the shiner?'

Stacy wheeled the pushchair inside and sat down at the kitchen table. 'His dad did it,' she said, flushing.

Appalled, Harriet added a dollop of cream to a mug of strong coffee and passed it to Stacy.

'Thanks.' The girl stirred sugar into the steaming liquid and sipped it gratefully. 'Yummy! I love real coffee.'

Harriet gave her a searching look. 'What happened, Stacy?'

'Greg came round last night when Mum was out, wanting to see Robert. He'd had a drink, so I wouldn't let him. We had a bit of a struggle when he tried to get past me and he caught me on the cheek with his elbow. So I told him to get lost.'

'I'm not surprised!'

'He didn't mean to hit me. He's not like that.' Stacy sighed, depressed. 'But I won't let him come near Robert if he's had a drink. I had enough of that with my own father. Not that Greg drinks much, he can't afford it, but he gets frustrated because he can't get a full-time job, and I won't get a place with him until he does.'

'How old is he?'

'Same age as me. I fell for Robert while Greg and I were still in school.' Stacy shrugged philosophically. 'At the moment cleaning is all I can do, but I go to computer classes two evenings a week, so by the time Robert starts nursery school I'll be able to try for office jobs.'

'How about Greg? Is he trained for anything?'

'He's got a couple of A-levels, but he likes to be out-doors, so he does whatever garden jobs he can get.'

'It's not easy for either of you, then,' said Harriet. 'Look, Stacy, there's no need for you to do any cleaning today—'

The girl eyed her in dismay. 'But I want to. *Please!* I'm sorry I had to bring Robert, but I couldn't leave him with Mum in case Greg came back. She'd have given him what for over my eye, and Robert gets terrified when people shout.'

'Bring Robert any time you like,' Harriet assured her. 'But for pity's sake take it easy. If you feel rough at any point pack it in.'

Robert woke up while his mother was finishing the sitting room. Stacy changed his nappy with swift efficiency, but when she fastened her son back in the buggy the move met with heartbroken protests.

'Why don't I take him out in the garden?' suggested Harriet. 'Would he like to sit on a blanket for a bit in the sun?'

'He'd just love it,' said Stacy, and kissed her son's wet cheeks as she popped a floppy cotton hat on his fair curls. 'Thanks, Harriet. I brought some toys for him to play with.'

There was a sticky moment when Stacy left her son with his new playmate, but Robert soon decided that he liked sitting on a rug in the sunshine. His tears dried like magic when Harriet began building a tower with plastic bricks. He scooted nearer, demolished them with chuckles of delight, and made imperious demands for a repeat perfor-mance. Harriet obeyed, laughing, time and time again, and felt quite sorry when Stacy came out at last to say she'd finished for the day.

'We've had a great time, Mummy.' With reluctance Harriet gave Robert to his mother. 'Are you going home now?'

'No, I'm due at the vicarage first.'

'Can you take Robert there with you?'

'I don't normally, but I'll just have to for once. I just hope the vicar isn't writing his sermon today.' She gave Harriet an uncertain smile. 'Would you mind if I gave Robert his lunch here, first?'

'Of course not. In fact,' added Harriet on impulse, 'why not leave him here with me afterwards?'

'I can't do that! It's taking advantage.'

'No, it's not. If he gets restless I'll take him for a walk in his buggy.'

'If you're really sure, that would be great,' said Stacy thankfully. 'I've got my phone, so just ring me if there's a problem.'

When his young mother left later Robert showed a moment of lip-trembling doubt when she kissed him goodbye, but he cheered up when his new friend took him back into the garden. Harriet built brick towers again for a while, but when the blue eyes began to droop she laid the little boy down on the blanket with his teddy, opened an umbrella to shade him from the sun, then stretched out beside him, content just to watch over the child as he fell asleep.

'Mum, Mum?' he sobbed when he woke up, and Harriet picked him up, cuddling him close.

'She won't be long, my darling,' she assured him. 'How about some juice?'

Blessing efficient Stacy for leaving a beaker of his favourite tipple ready in the kitchen, Harriet took the tearful little boy inside to find it, and cuddled him on her lap, deeply relieved when he stopped crying to drink.

'What a good boy you are,' she said fervently, and then sniffed at him in deep dismay. 'Now this,' she told him, 'is where you make allowances for an amateur, Robert Dyer. I've never changed a nappy before.'

He gurgled, and clutched a lock of her hair as she bent over him, but made no objection to lying on the changing mat his mother had left ready. Harriet had watched closely when Stacy changed her son, but in actual practice found that, like gardening, the process wasn't as easy as it looked. Due to much chuckling and wriggling it seemed a very long time before Robert was clean, fragrant and put back together again. Flushed with success, Harriet praised him extravagantly, balanced him inexpertly while she washed her hands, then sat him on her lap and gave him a biscuit.

'Where's Stacy?' demanded a voice from the open doorway.

Harriet jumped up in fright, clutching the child protectively at the sight of a thin, furious youth she'd never seen before.

Robert beamed, and the boy darted forward, arms outstretched.

'Hand him over!' he yelled.

Robert burst into tears at the loud noise, and burrowed his face against Harriet's neck.

'Who are you?' she demanded, her arms tightening round the child. 'What are you doing in my house?'

'I'm Greg Watts, Robert's dad. Give him to me!' He tried to snatch his child, but Robert held onto Harriet, sobbing piteously when he dropped his biscuit.

'Don't be an idiot, man,' she said, standing her ground. 'Can't you see you're frightening Robert to death? Stacy left him in my charge so I'm holding onto him until she comes back.'

'You've no right. I'm his *father*,' he said, his voice cracking, but as he made another lunge for the child James Devereux strode through the open door, seized Greg by the scruff of his neck and marched him outside, then came back to check on Harriet.

'Are you all right?' James demanded.

'I'm fine, but Robert's very upset.' She kissed the sobbing baby and cuddled him close. 'Oh, sweetheart, don't cry. I'll ring Mummy and ask her to come right now. James, you didn't hurt the boy, did you?' she said anxiously.

'Of course not. Greg says the child is his, but who's the mother?' he added.

'Stacy Dyer, my cleaner.'

'Give me the number and I'll ring her. Then I'll get Greg back in here and read the Riot Act.'

James' lecture was so effective Greg Watts was trying to choke back tears when Stacy raced in, wild-eyed and distraught.

'Greg, what on earth have you done?' she wailed.

The young man stared in horror at her bruised eye. 'Oh, God, Stace, did I do that? I'm *sorry*! You know I wouldn't hurt you for the world. I just wanted to see Robert.'

Much to Harriet's surprise the child had fallen asleep on her shoulder. 'He's fine,' she assured the girl, handing him over with care. 'He was a bit frightened by all the fuss, that's all.'

'Miss Dyer should really call in the police,' James told the boy sternly. 'You obviously intended to abduct the child.'

'*No!*' The boy stared at him in utter dismay. 'I just wanted to take Robert home to my mother for a bit, Mr Devereux. Stacy wouldn't let me near him last night.'

'If you behave like this I never will, either,' she snapped, glaring at him over her son's damp curls.

'Don't involve the police, love, *please*,' he pleaded. 'I'll never have a drink again if you let me see more of Robert. I'm not like your dad, Stacy, honest. I would never hurt you or my boy.'

She nodded slowly. 'I know that, Greg.'

There was silence for a moment while the young pair gazed at each other, oblivious of the other two.

'You can load the buggy in the car and I'll drive you

home, Stacy,' said Harriet at last, but the girl shook her head firmly.

'No way, Harriet. I'll wheel Robert, and Greg can carry my things.'

The boy's eyes lit up. 'Can I give Robert his tea?'

'Yes. And his bath, if you like.' She fastened her sleeping son in his pushchair, and turned to Harriet. 'After all this fuss do you still want me on Thursday?'

'Of course I do.'

'Thanks.' She eyed Harriet's pallor anxiously. 'You look shattered. I'd better make you some tea before I go.'

'No need, I'll do that,' said James quickly.

Stacy smiled shyly at him. 'OK, Mr Devereux. Come on, then, Greg.'

The boy looked at Harriet in remorse. 'I'm really sorry. I know Stacy works here on Mondays so I came round to apologise for last night. I didn't expect to find Robert here. When I saw him on your lap I just lost it.'

'Because Stacy left your son with a stranger instead of with you,' Harriet said with understanding.

'Which gave you no right to terrorise Miss Verney, my lad,' said James sternly.

'I know that, Mr Devereux.' Greg pulled a face. 'When Dad hears about this I'll probably get a shiner to match Stacy's.'

'He won't hear it from me,' James assured him, relenting.

When the young pair had finally departed with their son James drew out a chair. 'You look exhausted, Harriet. Sit down. Is there anything to drink in the house?'

'Wine in the fridge.'

'No brandy?'

'There might be some in the cabinet in the other room.' She got up, but James pushed her down again.

'I'll look.'

Surprised by an urge to lay her head down on the table and howl once she was alone, Harriet combed her fingers through her untidy hair, brushed soggy biscuit crumbs from her T-shirt, and managed a smile when James returned with a bottle of cognac and two crystal brandy snifters.

'My grandmother's emergency kit,' she informed him.

'I think we can definitely class this as an emergency.' He poured a small quantity into each glass and handed one over.

Harriet took a cautious sip from hers, shuddering a little as the fiery heat hit her. 'Thank you for coming to my rescue. Greg gave me rather a shock.'

James nodded. 'I know. That's why I was so rough with the kid.'

'It probably taught him a lesson.' Harriet smiled ruefully. 'When Stacy said the child's father had hit her I visualised some bruiser with fists like sledgehammers, so Greg came as something of a surprise. It was sad, really. Robert was delighted to see his daddy until Greg frightened him by yelling at me. How do you know Watts Senior, by the way?'

'You probably know him as Frank. He's the head gardener up at the house. I've known young Greg all his life.'

'His father must be good at his job. It all looked very perfect when I was up there the other day.' Harriet sighed. 'Poor Greg. I'm glad Stacy relented towards him.'

'Talking of relenting,' said James lightly, 'did you tell Tim you had lunch with me?'

'Yes. For once he was lost for words.' She grinned. 'I was pretty surprised myself.'

'That you shared a meal with the ogre and survived?'

Harriet flushed. 'I don't think of you as an ogre.'

'Liar!'

'All right, a bit, maybe. When I was young.'

'You're young now, Harriet.'

'Older than I was. You don't scare me any more.'

He frowned. 'Did I scare you in the past, then?'

'Of course you did!' She drained her glass. 'You blamed me every time Tim disobeyed your orders.'

'Because I knew he was obeying yours instead.'

'Mine were always suggestions, not orders.' Harriet gave him a straight look. 'And Tim only fell in with them when they appealed to him. You must surely know by now that he goes his own sweet way.'

'I do.' He got up. 'But in spite of that, or maybe because of it, I still feel protective towards him.'

'And you're convinced I'm going to hurt him in some way.' She looked at him challengingly. 'Do you really believe I'm sneaking into other men's beds behind Tim's back?'

His eyes flared dangerously for an instant. 'Are you?'

They stared at each other in taut silence for a moment.

'I don't have to answer to you, James,' she said hoarsely, and turned away.

He moved round the table and turned her face up to his. 'Tears, Harriet?'

She jerked her head away, blinking hard. 'Would you go now, please?'

'Harriet, I'm sorry. I've no right to question your private life,' he said wearily.

'No, you haven't.' Harriet reached blindly for a sheet of kitchen paper to mop herself up, and James caught her in his arms, pressing her face against his chest as he smoothed her hair.

'Don't cry, little one,' he said, in a tone that brought the tears on thick and fast. For a few blind, uncaring moments Harriet sobbed with abandon, but as she calmed down she grew aware of James' heart thudding against her own, and pulled away in panic.

'It's just reaction to all the drama,' she said thickly,

knuckling the tears away. 'Go away. I'd rather cry in private.'

'I'd rather you didn't cry at all,' he said huskily. 'Particularly when I'm to blame.'

She turned to face him, careless of tousled hair and swollen eyes. 'The man you saw with me at the theatre is an old college friend, and Tim was perfectly happy about it. It's absolutely none of your business, James Devereux, but just for the record I don't sleep around. Now let's drop the subject.'

For once James looked at a complete loss. 'Harriet—'

She held up an imperious hand. 'Look, I'm tired. Could you just go now?'

On his way to the door he paused, and turned to look at her. 'On an entirely different subject, Harriet, I need an assistant gardener to help Frank Watts. If I offered the job to his son, my bar manager could move here to End House and young Greg could take Stacy and the boy to the garage flat,' he added. 'Think about it. I'll be in touch.'

She stood utterly still for a while after he'd gone, staring at the door James had closed so gently behind him. Clever devil, she thought resentfully, then gave a wry little laugh. He might think he was persuading her in the one way certain of success, but he'd actually given her the perfect, face-saving way out of a dilemma. She could now sell End House at a very good price without revealing her change of heart. And no one need know that living alone there on a permanent basis had lost its appeal after only a day or two.

CHAPTER THREE

THE drama of the afternoon left Harriet with no enthusiasm for a trip to Cheltenham to see a film, as she'd intended. Instead she stretched out on the cane sofa in the conservatory after supper, trying to read. But, restless for reasons she refused to analyse, she gave up after a while and went out to water the flowers in the herbaceous borders instead. She spotted a gap in the hedge she hadn't noticed before, made a note to point it out to James and, reluctant to go back indoors on such a beautiful evening, she fetched her phone and sat on the rustic seat at the end of the garden to ring Dido.

'About time,' her friend said indignantly. 'Don't you ever look at your messages?'

'I've had distractions.' With suitable drama Harriet described her adventures of the afternoon.

'Wow!' said Dido, awed. 'You must have been scared to death.'

'Not really. He was only a kid. Anyway Tim's brother came charging to the rescue—'

'Are we talking the famous *Jed* here?'

'That's the one! He's down here doing staff interviews for Edenhurst.'

'And he just happened to be on hand in your hour of need? How come?'

'No idea. He was just passing, I suppose. What's new with you?'

In triumph Dido announced that she'd been given a pay rise, and told Harriet to be back in good time on Saturday.

'I'm in a party mood, so I've asked some people round to celebrate. Make sure Tim comes, too.'

After she'd rung off Harriet sat staring down the garden, not too thrilled about going back to plunge straight into one of her friend's parties. The flat would be filled to overflowing with glossy, perfectly groomed people who worked for the same famous cosmetics house as Dido. No one would leave until the small hours, and before getting to bed there would be an argument, as usual, when Harriet insisted the mess had to be cleared up first.

Then something Dido said came back to Harriet. Why *had* James appeared at her back door at just that particular moment? She curled a lock of hair round her finger as she tried to think of him objectively. If she'd met James Edward Devereux for the first time this week as a stranger, would she have been attracted to him on a purely man/woman basis? She bit her lip. She might have hero-worshipped him when she was a child, but she'd never thought of him in that way before, and right now the worrying answer was yes. Tim would laugh his head off when she told him—not that she would tell him. He wouldn't understand. Nor would she blame him. She didn't understand, either.

Harriet was on her way to bed when the phone rang, and because only one person ever rang her that late she chuckled as she lifted the receiver.

'Some people keep respectable hours, Tim Devereux.'

'Wrong brother, Harriet,' said James coolly.

'Oh—sorry. Hello.'

'I had a word with Frank Watts and told him that if Greg wanted a job I'd see him tomorrow afternoon. I made no mention of accommodation, obviously.'

'Will you give Greg the job even if I don't let you have End House?'

'Of course I will!' said James impatiently. 'I'm ringing

at this hour because it would obviously help if I knew your decision about the house before I see him, Harriet. Think about it overnight. I'll call round in the morning for your answer.'

Harriet locked up and went upstairs to lean out of the open bedroom window, the nostalgic, summer scent of roses reminding her that her grandmother would have strongly approved of James Devereux as the purchaser for End House. Olivia Verney had been very fond of Tim, but Harriet knew she'd had enormous respect for the brother who'd worked so hard to provide security for him.

Next morning Harriet was up early. After a shower she creamed her skin with one of the free samples that often came her way from Dido, brushed her hair until it shone, and instead of tying it back left it to cascade in loose waves to her shoulders. As the final touch she made her face up in City style, instead of the sole smear of moisturiser it had made do with since her arrival. Once she agreed to sell End House to James Devereux she might not see him again for ages and sheer pride urged her to leave him with a better impression than the tear-stained creature of yesterday.

The best Harriet could do from the limited choice of clothes she'd packed was a short ecru denim skirt and jacket and a vest top in a caramel shade that toned well with her hair. And instead of meekly waiting in for whenever James deigned to arrive she went on her usual trip to the shops to buy a paper and her daily pint of milk. She walked back slowly through sunshine that had a heavy, sultry feel to it, and found James, as she'd hoped, waiting on the rustic seat at the end of the garden, formal in a lightweight dark suit. He got up to take her carrier bag, and gave her a look that made all the primping and fussing worthwhile.

'Good morning, Harriet. You're obviously going somewhere.'

'I'm off to Cheltenham later on. I intended to yesterday, but after all the commotion I didn't feel like it. Do come in.' Harriet unlocked the door, switched on the kettle and motioned him to a seat at the table. 'I take it you'd like some coffee?'

'Thank you. How do you feel this morning? Any ill effects from yesterday's episode?'

'No.' This time she was ultra-careful as she poured boiling water into the cafetière. 'I'll leave the coffee to mature a bit,' she said, putting the tray on the table. 'But I'll get to the point right now. I accept your offer for End House. Your moral blackmail worked perfectly.'

The striking eyes narrowed as they met hers. 'Blackmail?'

She smiled cynically. 'You know exactly the right buttons to push, James Devereux. You knew I'd cave in once you brought Stacy and the baby into the equation.'

He made no attempt to deny it. 'But Greg may not accept the job,' he warned, 'and even if he does, Stacy may not join forces with him.'

'But my bank balance will look a lot healthier.' She looked at him thoughtfully. 'Why are you so keen to buy End House?'

'If you sold to someone else it might not be maintained to Edenhurst standards. I approached your grandmother about it some time ago,' he added, 'but she told me to wait until the house was yours.'

Harriet nodded sadly. 'She told me she was leaving it to me, but I couldn't bear to talk about it. When did she tell you?'

'I spotted your grandmother leaning against a farm gate at the entrance to Withy Lane one day when I was driving into the village. She accepted a ride with such relief I was worried. She was breathless and very pale, so I insisted on coming in the house with her. I wanted to call a doctor, but she wouldn't hear of it. She put a pill under her tongue, and after fixing me with those big dark eyes you inherited, she admitted that she had a heart problem, but threatened to come back and haunt me if I told anyone about it.'

Harriet stared at him, arrested. 'She knew she was ill as long ago as that?'

James nodded. 'She had such a fright that day she took me into her confidence. I learned that your parents had died too young to make much provision for you, but at least End House and its contents would be yours to dispose of as you wished one day, along with enough funds to keep it going for six months to give you time to decide what to do with it.'

'So you've known all along that the house would come to me,' said Harriet quietly.

He nodded. 'I knew the time was up about now, so once Tim told me you were spending the week here to make your decision I arranged the job interviews for the same time.'

'I see. But if you're in the middle of interviews how were you able to materialise at just the right moment yesterday?'

'I was next door, checking on repairs needed to the roof. When I heard shouting and a baby crying, I barged through the hedge to see what was going on.'

'So that's why there's a hole in it. I was going to report on that.' She looked at him curiously. 'Don't you employ people to inspect your property?'

'Of course I do. And in the others I leave the various estate managers to deal with it. It's different here on my home territory. I prefer a hands-on approach at Edenhurst.' James paused. 'Has Tim ever shown you the apartment I converted from the stable block?'

'No. On the rare occasions he's come down here with me he won't go near the house.'

James gave her a grim smile. 'If he wouldn't with you

for company, he never will with me. I suppose I should be grateful he likes my flat in London.'

'So much he could bore for Britain on the subject!'

'You never come there with him, Harriet, no matter how often I invite you. I suppose I can guess why.'

She flushed. 'Something else always seems to crop up.'

He smiled sardonically. 'No need to fudge, Harriet. Tim told me you weren't comfortable about coming to the ogre's lair.'

'He said that?'

'No, the choice of phrase is mine.' James gave her a straight look. 'Now we've agreed to a truce, will you come with him next time I ask?'

'All right.' Harriet hesitated for a moment. 'Look, James, if I ask you a question, will you tell me the truth, not just what you think I should know?'

'If I can,' he said warily.

'Tim said you were here in Upcote when my grandmother died.'

'Yes, I was.'

She looked at him in appeal. 'I've never liked to ask you before, but do you know what actually happened? I was on holiday in Scotland. My flatmate's parents own a cottage there. When I made it back here the vicar and his wife were very kind, but I had the feeling they were keeping something from me.'

His eyes softened. 'Then I can set your mind at rest. I was next door with Alec Price, the estate manager, when I saw your grandmother in the garden and went out to talk over the hedge about her problem with moles. She was concerned about a cough I'd developed and told me to go home and take a hot toddy. She breathed in sharply mid-sentence, said she felt dizzy, and quietly fainted. Or so I thought. I vaulted over the hedge in my rush to get to her, and Alec called an ambulance. But when the paramedics arrived they couldn't revive her. She'd gone.' James reached for Harriet's hand, his eyes warm with compassion. 'She died in exactly the place she'd have chosen,' he said gently. 'One minute she was right here in the garden she loved, the next she was with the angels.'

'Thank you,' said Harriet gruffly, when she could trust her voice. 'It's a relief to know the truth.'

James looked at his watch and dropped her hand. 'Damn. I'd better run.'

Harriet got up quickly. 'Hang on a minute. What must I do to get the ball rolling about the sale?'

'Come up to the house this evening. We can discuss it over dinner.'

She shook her head. 'No, thanks. Could you just pop back here for a few minutes?'

His eyes frosted. 'As you wish, Harriet, but it may be late.'

'Whenever.'

Harriet felt a twinge of remorse after James left. She knew she'd offended him, but sheer vanity had prompted her refusal. For a formal place like the Edenhurst dining room she had nothing suitable to wear. Unless, she thought suddenly, he'd meant supper alone with him in the stable flat.

Harriet caught a bus to Cheltenham for lunch and window-shopping, bought a cuddly lion for Robert and, because her finances would be in good shape once James Devereux paid her for End House, had a look round the sales and bought a dress to put her in the mood for Dido's party.

Tim rang when she got back.

'Hi,' said Harriet. 'How's gay Paree?'

'Fabulous! After I sorted the business part with my artist we visited loads of galleries, including the Louvre, of course, and did tourist things together like the Eiffel Tower, and a boat trip along the Seine, and much wining and dining and so on. Anyway, enough about fascinating *moi*, how's life in peaceful Upcote?'

'Not all that peaceful.' Harriet related her adventures with baby Robert and his parents, and surprised Tim by her description of James' way of dealing with the situation.

'Did he beat the bloke up?' said Tim, dumbfounded.

'Of course not. He just took him by the collar and frog-marched him outside.'

'And how, my angel, did Jed just happen to be on hand to rescue you?'

'He was next door and heard the noise. The boy was shouting and the baby was crying—'

'Stop! Go back to London at once. It's obviously far too dangerous in Upcote. Anyway, I want you waiting with open arms to greet the returning wanderer.'

'Of course. By the way,' she added casually, 'I've sold the house. Your brother's bought it as digs for the Edenhurst bar manager.'

'Has he really?' said Tim slowly. 'At one time you clammed up and went all hoity-toity if I even mentioned big brother's name, but if you've let him have the house you've obviously thawed towards him quite a bit.'

'He thought you'd be pleased.'

'I am, in a way.' There was a pause. 'But for obvious reasons don't get *too* chummy with Jed.'

'Of course I won't,' she said scornfully. 'You have nothing to fear, Timothy Devereux.'

'Good.' He sighed. 'I miss you, Harry.'

'I miss you, too. Have fun, I'll see you soon—must go, there's someone at the door. Bye.'

Her visitors were Stacy and Greg, their faces incandescent with excitement as they gave her their news.

'We just had to come and tell you, Harriet,' said Stacy breathlessly.

'The garage flat goes with the job!' Greg added. 'We're going to live together at last, and be a proper family for Robert.'

Harriet congratulated the jubilant young pair and saw them off, glad that something rather wonderful had come from her decision to sell End House.

It was after nine by the time James arrived, looking a lot more approachable in thin cotton trousers and rolled-up shirtsleeves.

'Sorry I'm late. I got held up.' He handed her a chilled bottle. 'I brought some champagne to celebrate our deal. Or have you changed your mind since I saw you last?'

'Of course not. Stacy and Greg came round earlier.' Harriet smiled as she produced glasses. 'They were so happy, it scotched any doubts I had about parting with End House.'

James chuckled as he eased the cork from the bottle of champagne. 'I thought young Greg was going to pass out from excitement when I told him a flat went with the job.'

'You must have felt like God!'

'Not quite.' He shot her a look. 'If I had even a trace of that kind of power I'd have organised some things in my life very differently, my marriage included.'

Harriet pulled a face as she accepted a glass of champagne. 'The last time that subject was mentioned you changed it pretty sharply.'

'And spoilt our surprisingly amicable lunch,' he agreed. 'But as you know, Harriet, my wife left me for the all-too-common reason that she met someone else.'

'Tim was delighted about that. He didn't care for her at all.'

'Poor Madeleine. She believed that her looks were all she had to offer. When new young faces began to replace hers on magazine covers the punishing diet and constant beauty treatments weren't enough any more. When she started on cosmetic surgery I blew the whistle, so she left me.' James drank his champagne down and refilled both glasses.

'That's my limit,' warned Harriet. 'Any more and I'll be telling you the story of my life.'

'That's only fair in return for mine.' His lips twitched. 'Although I know most of yours already.'

Not everything, thought Harriet thankfully. 'Is Madeleine happy with the new husband?'

'No idea. After she walked out all communications were made through lawyers.'

'Talking of lawyers, what happens next about the house?'

James spent a few minutes discussing the opening moves in the transaction, and then asked to see over the house to assess any work needed.

'I'm not quite sure what I should do about the furniture,' Harriet told him when they went into the sitting room. 'I want things like the porcelain for keepsakes, obviously, but I can't see the furniture fitting in anywhere I'm likely to live.'

'No,' James agreed. 'Tim's taste runs to the strictly con-temporary. I suggest you make a list of the things you really like, and I'll send the rest to Dysart's Auction House in Pennington.'

'That's very kind of you,' said Harriet, wincing when lightning flashed as she went ahead of him up the narrow stairs.

'I *can* be kind,' he said dryly.

'Greg and Stacy can testify to that.'

'I meant to you, Harriet.'

She turned away to show him the smaller bedroom, which had been furnished specifically for her when she was thirteen. The only thing missing was the battered teddy bear she'd left behind in London.

'I decided to sleep in my grandmother's bed this time in

case I never had the chance again,' Harriet told James as she took him into the main bedroom. 'The armoire would be a bit overpowering in a flat, but I'll keep the brass bed and the Georgian chest. It's beautiful, isn't it?' she added wistfully.

'This must be very painful for you, Harriet,' said James with sympathy.

'A bit, but it has to be done.' She blinked hard. 'Sorry. Champagne makes me emotional. And I'm not terribly keen on storms, either.'

Harriet gave a stifled little squeak as thunder cracked overhead, and James took her in his arms. 'Nothing to be afraid of,' he said soothingly.

He was wrong. Just to be held close to him like this was terrifying because she liked it so much. Hardly daring to breathe, Harriet stood utterly still as his arms tightened round her. Her palms grew damp and her breath caught in her throat when she looked up to meet shock in James' eyes. He stared down at her for a breathless interval, as though he'd never seen her before, and Harriet stared back, mesmerised, as he slowly bent his head to kiss her. When their lips met, hers parted in a gasp, his arms tightened, his tongue slid into her mouth and he held her hard against him, kissing her with such sudden, explicit hunger her knees buckled and she collapsed on the bed. James followed her down, his mouth and hands undermining her resistance so completely it took a crack of thunder to bring Harriet down to earth. She gave a smothered choke of disbelief and tore herself from his arms to stand at the far side of the bed, head averted, clutching at the carved brass finial of the bed as she tried to get her breath back.

Eyes tight shut, Harriet willed James to go away, but he moved round the foot of the bed to raise her face to his.

'Open your eyes! I'm not going to attack you again.'

She raised her lids to half-mast and heaved in a deep breath. 'It was just a kiss.'

'It felt like a hell of a lot more than that to me.' He stared down at her in dazed disbelief.

'It was just a kiss,' she insisted.

His eyes narrowed dangerously. 'Like this?' he said through his teeth, and caught her in his arms again. Harriet struggled for an instant, but he held her still and the fight went out of her, replaced by something that surged through her entire body, and frightened her to death. Pure, unadulterated lust was something new in her life, but in response to James Devereux's relentless hands and mouth she shook and burned with it, and felt answering heat scorch from his body into hers before he thrust her away with a groan of self-loathing.

'What the hell am I *doing*?'

'Conducting an experiment, maybe?' Harriet spat at him, shaking her hair back.

The heat faded from his eyes. 'What do you mean?'

She heaved in a deep, unsteady breath. 'I told you I didn't sleep around. Maybe you were putting me to the test.'

All expression drained from James Devereux's face. 'No,' he said slowly. 'Tests imply conscious thought. I just wanted you, Harriet. God help me, I still do.'

She rubbed a hand across her damp forehead, feeling her resentment evaporate at his honesty. '*Why?* We don't even like each other very much.'

He smiled bleakly. 'Our hormones obviously don't believe that.' The smile vanished suddenly. 'Will you tell Tim?'

Harriet shuddered. 'I most certainly will not. Will you?'

'Hell, no! I was the one spouting fine words about shielding Tim from hurt.' His mouth twisted. 'We just forget it ever happened.'

'Right.'

His eyes held hers. 'I'm not sure I can do that.'

Harriet wasn't sure she could, either. 'It probably wouldn't have happened normally, but you were talking about Madeleine, and I was tearful about this place, and the storm didn't help—'

'None of which is anything to do with it. With you in my arms I forgot everything and everyone, including Tim. Laugh if you like,' he added savagely.

She shivered. 'I don't feel like laughing.'

'Neither do I. For God's sake let's get out of here, away from this bed.' He held the door open for her and Harriet brushed past, trying not to touch him as she made for the stairs.

In the kitchen, with the table between them and the storm retreating now in the distance, she felt marginally calmer as she faced the tall, haggard man who had just turned her life upside down.

'I'll ring my grandmother's solicitor tomorrow.'

James nodded brusquely. 'If you'll give me the number I'll pass it on to my lawyer.'

'And until the sale is official I'll keep paying Stacy to clean the house,' said Harriet, determinedly matter-of-fact.

James shook his head. 'I'll see to that. She can carry on working here after the house changes hands. I'll talk to the Edenhurst housekeeper, too. There may be something Stacy can do up at the hotel on a regular basis.'

'Thank you. That would be a great help for her.'

Rain hammered against the window, and thunder cracked and rolled, but neither of them noticed the elements as silence fell that neither of them was willing to break. Harriet waited, nerves jumping, half wanting James to go and half wanting, quite desperately, for him to stay.

At last he gave her a look that turned her heart over.

'Tell me the truth, Harriet. If you and I were unconnected in any way, would you have let me stay tonight?'

'I would have wanted to,' she said honestly.

His eyes lit with triumph for an instant before the shutters came down. 'But because of Tim it will never happen.'

Harriet glared at him. 'I don't want to talk about Tim right now.'

'Let's talk about us instead, then.'

'There *is* no us, James.'

He moved round the table. 'So we simply delete the episode from our minds, forget it ever happened.'

'Yes,' she said gruffly, backing away. 'That's exactly what we do.'

James looked down at her for a moment, then caught her by the shoulders and kissed her so hard she was shaken and breathless when he thrust her away from him at last. 'Something else to delete,' he said savagely and went out into the rain, slamming the door behind him.

CHAPTER FOUR

NEXT morning Harriet rang Stacy with a change of plans. 'I'm leaving today after all. I've sold the house to Mr Devereux, and he'll be paying you from now on. Thank you for all your good work for me, Stacy. Would Greg see to the garden in his spare time until the property changes hands? I'll pay him the going rate.'

'Of course. He'll be only too glad to, Harriet. Will you come down here again?'

'Possibly. I'm not sure. By the way, I bought a little present for Robert yesterday, and in all the excitement forgot to give it to you last night. I've left it on the kitchen table. Give him a big kiss for me.'

'That's so sweet of you, Harriet. Thank you. Please come back and see us sometime.'

Harriet promised she would, then sent text messages to Dido and Tim, saying she'd be returning that day. She checked the house to make sure she'd left nothing behind, locked the familiar door and took her belongings out to the waiting taxi. As it drove away she looked back at End House with a sudden, sharp pang of misgiving, hoping she'd made the right decision.

When she let herself into the flat at lunchtime it was quiet, and remarkably tidy. Impressed, she took her bags into her room and unpacked the cushion bought in Cheltenham as a present for her friend. She went into Dido's room to leave it on the bed, and dodged out again in a hurry. Her friend was still in bed, and she had company.

Harriet sighed. She was fond of Dido, but this particular

aspect of sharing with her had its drawbacks. It was embarrassing, but not unusual, to run into one of Dido's men friends outside the bathroom of a morning, but normally only at weekends. Sleepovers before a working day were a first. Harriet retreated to her room to unpack, then curled up with the daily paper bought on the way and had finished the crossword by the time Dido tapped on the door.

'You can come out now. He's gone.'

Her face wan under a fall of silky fair hair, Dido smiled guiltily when Harriet joined her in the tiny kitchen. 'It's been lonely without you. Welcome back. Shall I throw some lunch together?'

'Sure you're not too tired?' Harriet batted her eyelashes. 'Sorry I disturbed love's young dream. I backed out in a hurry—honest.'

But there was no answering smile from Dido as she buttered bread. 'I didn't expect you back so early. Not that it matters, you know it wasn't Tim—not that I'd ever try to poach on your preserves,' she added hastily.

'Whose *were* you poaching on, then?'

'Nobody's as far as I know. Louise from Regional Sales brought her brother to the pub to meet the rest of us for her birthday bash last night. He gave me a lift home, and it's my day off today—'

'So he stayed the night,' said Harriet, resigned.

'Why not?' said Dido, flushing. 'It's different for you. You've got Tim.'

'I go out with other men occasionally.'

'But you don't sleep with them. For you there's only Tim. I don't have anyone like that in my life.'

'Oh, come *on*, you know loads of men.'

'No one who matters—' Dido's head flew up in consternation as the buzzer sounded.

'Don't worry. If it's your mystery lover back for seconds I'll see him off. Hide in the bathroom.'

Harriet picked up the receiver and pressed the release button, and smiled, delighted, when she heard a familiar voice. Tim came in like a whirlwind, brandishing a carrier bag, grinning all over his face.

'Great—you're here already. I come with gifts, angel. Will you feed me, or are you entertaining a lover behind my back?'

'Not today,' said Harriet, engulfed in a bear hug. 'I didn't expect you so early. Have you come straight from Waterloo?'

'I sure have, and I'm hungry.'

'What a surprise! Ask Dido nicely and she'll probably let you have something.'

'And where is the fair Dido?' asked Tim, wolfing a piece of bread.

'In the bath, I think.'

He went to hammer on the bathroom door. 'Come out, Dido. I've brought you a present, and I'm starving.'

'Be gentle with her,' said Harriet when he rejoined her. 'She's just got out of bed.'

He grinned. 'Don't worry, I shall handle her with kid gloves—or maybe not. She might like it too much.'

She laughed, admiring the new jacket and stylish haircut. 'You look good. You obviously had a great time?'

'The best. How did you survive your stay in Upcote?'

'By leaving in a hurry.'

'As bad as that?' The familiar Devereux eyes narrowed on hers. 'You shall tell me all later—ah!' He turned as Dido, fully dressed and face perfect, rushed in to kiss him.

'So what did you get up to in Paris, then, Tim Devereux?' she demanded.

'I'll tell you over lunch if you'll give me some food.' He smiled coaxingly as he handed her a package. 'I brought you some perfume guaranteed to send men wild with lust.'

Tim lifted Dido's mood, as usual, but after the meal she bestowed a valiant little smile on him and got up to go.

'I know you want to catch up with Harriet so I'll pop out to do some shopping. See you later.'

'What's up with Goldilocks?' asked Tim, after she'd gone.

Harriet sighed. 'A man stayed the night.'

'Not that unusual for Dido?'

'It was someone she'd just met. Again. She worries me lately. She's so desperate to find a man like you.'

'Like *me*?'

'I mean someone special in her life. She's been detoxing, botoxing, having her teeth whitened, eyelashes dyed, and heaven knows what else.'

Tim eyed her closely. 'You don't do her kind of thing, do you?'

'Invite strange men to stay the night?'

'I meant the drastic beauty stuff.'

'A bit of basic maintenance, otherwise what you see is what you get.' She wagged a finger. 'But don't play the innocent. You know perfectly well that Dido's got a crush on you.'

'And you know perfectly well why she's on a losing wicket.' Tim drew Harriet down on the sofa, eyeing her sternly. 'Don't beat yourself up over Dido. It's her life.'

'I know.' She grinned at him. 'Now tell me what you really got up to on your trip.'

Half an hour later, when he was on the point of leaving, Tim remembered to ask what else had happened in Upcote.

'Nothing much,' she said casually, her stomach churning at the lie. 'I had a couple of lazy days down there, then sold End House to your brother.'

'At a cracking good price, I hope.'

'Since you ask, yes.' Harriet sighed. 'I didn't need much

time to sort things out, after all. It's a pity I docked a whole week from the Italian trip.'

'You'll still have a fortnight.'

'Can't wait!'

Tim smiled at her in approval. 'You obviously got on a bit better with Jed if you let him have your beloved house.'

'We agreed to a truce. But he strongly disapproves of my friendships with other men.' She looked him in the eye. 'He's afraid I'll hurt you.'

Tim shrugged. 'Jed just can't help feeling protective, love. Besides, I know you'll never hurt me.'

'Try telling your brother that,' she said tartly.

Tim tapped her cheek with his forefinger. 'Why is he always *my brother*? Can't you force yourself to say his name?'

'I'm never going to call him Jed. But I try to manage his given name now and then. It's part of the new peace-keeping treaty. Which I agreed to solely to make you happy,' she added, not quite truthfully.

'You always make me happy.' He held out a hand to pull her to her feet and held her close. 'I missed you, Harry.'

'I missed you, too.' She held her face up for his kiss. 'I'm glad you had a good time.'

'I know you are.' He stroked her hair gently.

She smiled and patted his cheek. 'Now go home and get to bed early, you look tired. By the way, Dido's throwing a party next Saturday. You're invited.'

'Of course I am. Tell her I accept with pleasure.' Tim clapped a hand to his forehead, and took a package from his holdall. 'I almost forgot. I brought boring scent for Dido, but for you something special.'

Harriet tore open the wrappings to find sexy wisps of underwear, with a label that made her mouth water. 'Tim, you extravagant thing, they're gorgeous, *and* the right size!

Thank you. I'll wear them under my new dress at Dido's soirée.'

But after Harriet had been through Dido's strict cleanse/tone/moisturise routine before the party a few days later it was James she thought of as she made up her face. The caramel brown of her long, waving hair was natural, the shape under her new dress was all her own, and the effect was satisfactory even to her own critical eyes. She blew a kiss of approval to her reflection. He wouldn't be there to notice, but even by James Devereux's exacting standards the ugly duckling was quite a presentable swan these days.

Tim was still missing by the time the flat was packed to the doors with Dido's guests.

'Where is he?' muttered Dido impatiently as they opened more bottles in the kitchen.

'He'll be here soon,' Harriet assured her.

But when Tim finally put in an appearance he had company.

'Hi, gorgeous,' he said, kissing Harriet. 'Jed called in to see me just as I was leaving, so he gave me a lift.'

'Why, hello,' said Harriet, wanting to clout Tim with one of the bottles he was carrying. 'This is a delightful surprise. I'll fetch Dido.'

'I'll do that.' Tim gave her a guilty look, and plunged into the crowd with his offerings like a criminal bent on escape.

As well he might, thought Harriet, simmering.

'I can leave right now, if you like,' offered James dryly, but Dido raced up to gush over him, and press him to a drink.

'How lovely to meet you at last,' she cried. 'I've heard so much about you.'

'And I about you,' he said, smiling down at her in a way that won him such a delighted, flirtatious response only the arrival of more guests forced Dido to tear herself away.

James moved close to Harriet at once, like a hunter closing in for the kill. 'Tim insisted I come in for a minute to say hello.'

'Surely you've got better things to do,' she muttered.

'I wanted to see you,' he said in a fierce undertone. 'I called round to End House next morning but the bird had flown.'

'It seemed like a good idea. This,' she added rapidly, 'is a bad one.'

'I need to talk to you.'

Harriet backed away. 'If it's about the house—'

'What are you two arguing about?' demanded Tim, putting an arm round her shoulders.

'We're discussing End House,' she told him.

'I was just asking Harriet to meet me sometime to go over the details regarding furniture, and so on,' said James casually.

'Good idea,' agreed Tim, delighted. 'The three of us could have lunch together tomorrow.'

'Come to the flat,' James said promptly. 'I'll organise a meal.'

'All right with you, love?' said Tim eagerly.

'Fine,' she assured him, resigned.

'I'll see you tomorrow, then, about one,' said James. 'Say my goodbyes to the hostess, Tim. Harriet, perhaps you'd see me out.'

She went out into the hall, and closed the door on the uproar in the flat. James stood close in silence, his eyes so like and yet so unlike Tim's, holding hers captive for a moment before he said the last thing she'd expected to hear. 'You look beautiful, Harriet.'

'Why, thank you.' She smiled challengingly. 'You like my swan outfit, then.'

'You were never an ugly duckling,' he said instantly. 'Robert loves the lion, by the way.'

'You've seen him?'

'Stacy brought him with her when she came to see the garage flat.' He moved closer. 'We need to talk alone, Harriet. Just tell me where and when and I'll meet you somewhere.'

She shook her head. 'No need. I'll just come to your place a few minutes early tomorrow.'

He raised a disbelieving black eyebrow. 'Ah, but will you break the habit of a lifetime and actually turn up this time?'

'Yes,' she said curtly.

'Good. I'll be waiting. Goodnight, Harriet.'

James gave her a formal, unsmiling bow and left, taking Harriet's zest for the party with him. Feeling oddly flat, she went to rescue Tim from a trio of Dido's colleagues, and agreed gratefully when he suggested taking food and a bottle of wine to her room to enjoy their own private party. But when they stole away with their feast they found Harriet's bed occupied.

'That does it,' said Harriet savagely, slamming the door shut. 'I just have to get a place of my own.'

'We could go back to mine,' suggested Tim, once he'd stopped laughing.

She shook her head. 'It's late and I'm hungry. Let's just sit out in the back area to eat this lot, and hope it doesn't rain!'

As Tim was leaving, Harriet reminded him about their lunch date next day. 'But there's no point in your trekking here to pick me up tomorrow. I'll meet you at your brother's place.'

Tim eyed her accusingly. 'Does that mean you're going to duck out of it as usual?'

'Certainly not. I have things to discuss with your—'

'For God's sake call him by his name,' he said irritably.

'All right, crosspatch. Go home to bed.'

Tim grinned penitently and gave her a hug. 'Goodnight, love. See you tomorrow.' He kissed her, drew back to yawn, and trudged off to the main entrance. He turned to look at her. 'By the way, did I tell you that you look pretty damn scrumptious tonight, Harry?'

'No, you didn't. But others did!'

It was three in the morning before the last reveller had left, and for once Dido began tidying up without argument.

'Tim left very early tonight,' she complained, emptying ashtrays into a bin bag. 'By the way, the famous Jed's a bit gorgeous! Why didn't he stay?'

'No idea. By the way, Tim and I are having lunch with him tomorrow.'

Dido gave her a cynical look. 'But are you actually turning up this time?'

'We've got a few loose ends to tie up over End House, so I have to.' Harriet yawned. 'Right, I'll leave you to the rest while I change my sheets for the second time in one day. I took Tim off to my room to eat our supper in peace, and walked in on a couple writhing about on my nice clean bed.'

'Oh, God, that's horrible!' Dido shuddered. 'What did you do?'

'Nothing. We shut the door on them and took our supper outside. It could have been worse. It's a fine night.'

'I'm so sorry!'

'Not your fault.'

Dido sighed as she began thumping sofa cushions. 'I suppose that settles it, especially now you've sold your grandma's house. You want a place of your own right away.'

'Yes, I do,' admitted Harriet. 'Can you manage the mortgage yourself, or will you get someone else to share?'

'I'll be fine now I've had a pay rise.' Dido collected a

few glasses, her face still averted. 'Are you and Tim going to move in together, then?'

'Not yet. I quite fancy being on my own for a while.'

'When you could be sharing with Tim? You're mad!'

The prospect of lunch next day gave Harriet another of the restless nights plaguing her lately. Seeing James Devereux, unexpected and out of context, had shaken her badly, and he'd known it.

It was raining hard next morning, which gave Harriet the perfect excuse to dress down in khaki combats and black ribbed cotton sweater, to make it clear she didn't look on the occasion as special. From the first day of James' move, Tim had driven her mad with constant descriptions of his brother's flat, which overlooked the Thames and occupied two floors of a redbrick Victorian warehouse James Devereux and his partner Nick Mayhew had transformed into luxury apartments.

Harriet paid off the taxi and dashed through the rain into the foyer to take the lift to the fourth floor. By the time she reached it she had her smile firmly in place when James, in jeans and chambray shirt, opened his door.

'So you actually came, Harriet. Welcome.' He stood aside to let her in. 'Let me take your umbrella.'

Harriet's tension vanished at first sight of the apartment. The glazed brickwork and great arched windows of the original building housed an interior that looked like a film set for a science fiction movie. Semi-circular white sofas were grouped with glass tables and steel lamps to face a huge plasma-screen television with free-standing speakers, the white, steel and glass theme continued in a kitchen and dining area dominated, like the entire, light-filled living space, by panoramic views of the river.

'Are you going to say something soon?' said James, amused.

'It's not a lot like Edenhurst.'

'True,' he agreed. 'What's your verdict?'

'For once Tim wasn't exaggerating,' she said obliquely, and walked to one of the windows to look at the spectacular view. 'Isn't it a bit like living in a goldfish bowl?'

'I had fine-slat blinds fitted in the bedroom—though only a passing seagull could look in. Let me give you a drink,' said James. 'I've got champagne on ice—'

'No, thanks,' she said, so vehemently he took her by the hand and turned her to face him.

'Relax, child.'

Harriet shook her head. 'I'm not a child any more.'

'No. It would be much simpler if you were.' He dropped her hand. 'So what can I offer you?'

She took a glass of fruit juice with her as he showed her the rest of the apartment. In the sparsely furnished bedroom Harriet gave a fleeting glance at the huge white-covered bed and looked round curiously. 'Where's your bathroom?'

'Through here.' James slid back an opaque glass panel behind the bed to reveal a mosaic-tiled shower, oval bath, and custom-made units in the glass, white and steel of the rest of the apartment. 'Would you like to stay here by yourself for a moment?' he asked tactfully.

'No, thanks,' she said, red-faced again, and splashed fruit juice down his chest in her haste to get away.

James grabbed a towel to blot his shirt, rolling his eyes. 'Harriet, for God's sake stop this sacrificial lamb act. I am not about to throw you on the floor and ravish you.' He gave her a sudden smile. 'Not that the idea lacks a certain appeal.'

Harriet let out a shamefaced little laugh. 'Sorry! Have I ruined your shirt?'

'No. Have a look at the rest of the flat, then we'll have this talk of ours before Tim gets here.' He looked at his watch. 'He can't be too much longer.' But while James was showing her the gadgets in his kitchen the phone rang.

'Tim? What's up? You sound rough.' James listened closely, his face inscrutable. 'In that case,' he said at last, 'take some pills and stay in bed to get in shape for work tomorrow. I'll hand you over to Harriet.'

'Hey,' she said, heart sinking. 'What's wrong?'

'I rang the flat but Dido said you'd left. I tried your phone, but no luck. Did you forget to charge it?' demanded Tim.

'I must have. Sorry.'

'Anyway, now I've tracked you down I'm grovelling. I feel like death. I had a drink or three with the others when I got home last night. Bad move. I told Jed I had a migraine, but for your ears only it's the father of all hangovers. Sorry, angel. I just can't make it today.'

'OK. Drink plenty of water, and get some sleep,' she said, resigned. 'Take care. I'll ring you tonight.'

'Shall I call a cab, or can I persuade you to stay to lunch?' James asked.

Harriet thought about it. 'I'll stay. But just for lunch.'

'Not for the orgy afterwards?' he said affably.

'Or maybe I'll stick with the cab,' she said, glaring at him.

He held up a hand. 'Let me give you lunch first.'

They sat at the table with the view to eat cold roast guinea fowl, served with a green salad and hunks of coarse, crusty bread.

'I kept it simple. This is the food I'd originally planned for my own lunch,' James told her, and filled their wineglasses. 'And it's just a New Zealand Sauvignon, not champagne.'

Harriet shot him a rueful look as she buttered her bread. 'This is funny, really. Tim not turning up, I mean. It's usually me.'

James' eyes gleamed. 'Come clean, Harriet. Tim's migraine is really a hangover, right?'

Harriet grinned. 'Afraid so. I suppose he thought big brother would be angry if he told the truth.'

'Most people get hung-over sometime. Why should I be angry?'

'Because I turned up at last and he didn't. Tim feels guilty.'

'So do I.'

'Why?'

He looked her in the eye. 'Because I'm enjoying the unexpected treat of lunching alone with you. A stupid thing to admit, because you'll probably go rushing off right away.'

Harriet shook her head. 'We're supposed to talk,' she reminded him. 'It's my reason for coming here.'

'Right up to the moment I opened my door to you I was sure you wouldn't,' he told her.

'So was I,' she said frankly. 'But I promised Tim.'

'Why else?' he said, resigned, and refilled their glasses. 'You haven't told me yet what you think of the apartment.'

'It's not exactly cosy,' she said warily.

'It's not meant to be. It's a showcase, designed to demonstrate to prospective clients exactly what can be achieved with this kind of conversion. But go on,' he added. 'Tell me the worst.'

'It's not my cup of tea,' she said, turning to look at him. 'I admire it enormously as a concept. But it's too hard-edged for me. I couldn't live in it.'

'Tim would move in tomorrow.'

'So he's told me—ad nauseam.'

James laughed as he got up to take their plates. 'It's reassuring to know that you two don't agree on everything.' He put cheese and fruit on the table and sat down again. 'Right, then, Harriet. Let's talk furniture. I suggest you simply list what you want from End House, and I'll buy the rest from you.'

Harriet's eyes widened. 'For your bar manager?'

'No, he'll move his own things in. Have you decided what you want?'

'Just the Georgian chest and the china cabinet and its contents, and the brass bed,' she said, keeping her eyes on the orange she was peeling.

'The armoire and the lacquer fire screen would look perfect in my flat at Edenhurst, so I'll keep them myself,' said James, 'and I'll let Stacy and Greg have the rest. Is that agreeable to you?'

'It's a brilliant idea!' Harriet smiled at him warmly. 'My grandmother would be very pleased.'

'Are you?'

She nodded. 'Yes.'

'I'll give you a fair price—'

'Have everything valued first and then tell me what the professional thinks is a fair price,' she said firmly.

His eyes narrowed dangerously. 'Are you afraid I'll cheat you?'

'Of course not,' she said impatiently. 'I'm afraid you'll pay me over the odds, out of charity, like the offer for End House.'

'I'm a businessman. I don't deal in charity. My offer was exactly what the house is worth,' said James brusquely. 'And if you doubt my word about the furniture get the valuation done yourself.'

CHAPTER FIVE

HARRIET looked at James in dismay for a moment, then abandoned her orange and stood up.

'You're offended. I'm sorry. I was trying to say I don't expect any special treatment because—'

'Of what happened between us at End House?' he demanded, jumping to his feet. 'You think I'm finding a way to pay you money for that? It was something to forget, you told me, not something to pay for.'

'You know I didn't mean that,' Harriet said furiously. 'I meant my connection to Tim!'

'My brother,' said James, stalking round the table, 'is nothing to do with it.'

'Of course he is. I wouldn't be here otherwise,' she snapped, and stood her ground.

'You think I don't know that?' He stopped dead, inches away from her.

They stood erect and bristling, glittering tawny eyes boring down into resentful dark ones. Then James sighed, and gave her a wry smile.

'This is ridiculous. I just want you to have the best price possible, Harriet.'

'So that Tim and I can set up house together?'

He frowned. 'You said that wasn't in the cards yet.'

'It's not.'

'Good.'

Harriet raised a suspicious eyebrow. 'Why is it good?'

James took her by the hand and led her over to one of the curved white sofas. 'Let's sit down for a moment, Harriet, while we discuss certain inescapable facts of life.'

She tensed. 'What do you mean?'

'We both love Tim,' he stated.

'Yes.'

'But you do realise that he's the eternal Peter Pan?'

'Of course I do,' said Harriet, relaxing slightly. 'After all, he's only twenty-three.'

'So are you.'

'The female of the species matures faster than the male.' She smiled. 'Don't worry. I've no intention of trying to make Tim settle down yet. I just want a place of my own for a while. Particularly after last night.'

'What happened?'

Harriet explained, keeping her eyes on St Paul's in the distance, then turned to him wrathfully. 'You may well sit there grinning, but I'd only just changed the bed.'

'The last straw!' he agreed.

'It was the ultimate embarrassment as well.'

'I can imagine. The act of love is not a spectator sport.'

'We didn't stop to watch!' Suddenly Harriet's sense of humour revived. 'Tim thought it was hilarious,' she admitted, and they laughed together for a moment.

'I'm sorry I barked at you about the money, Harriet,' said James eventually. 'But when it comes to pushing buttons you're no slouch yourself.'

'I know. Sorry.'

'I promise I'll send you an itemised copy of Adam Dysart's valuation.'

'Thank you.' She held out her hand. 'Shall we shake on it?'

James took the hand in his, but instead of shaking it he raised it to his lips, and Harriet leapt up as though he'd scorched her.

'Hell, Harriet,' he growled, 'will you stop it?'

She flushed. 'Sorry. I'm just—tired. We spent hours tidying up after the party.'

'If your friend entertains on a regular basis I see why you want a place of your own,' he said dryly. 'I'll make some coffee.'

'Thank you.'

While they drank it Harriet gave James a brief account of her work as assistant to the junior director of a City head-hunting firm, smiling as she told him that Giles Kemble had been reluctant to let her have that particular week off for her trip to Upcote.

'Giles lives in a flat with a view of the London Eye. He thought I was raving mad to bury myself in the country on my own for even a day, let alone a week.'

'You ran away long before the week was up,' James reminded her.

Her chin lifted. 'I did not run away. Once the sale of End House was settled there was nothing to keep me there.'

'Of course you ran away. You were afraid I'd come back to take up where we left off.'

'Certainly not,' she lied. 'I knew you wouldn't do that.'

'I wish I shared your conviction.' His eyes held hers. 'I wanted to, Harriet. But I didn't, for obvious reasons. Not that you would have let me in. Last night you made it clear that you'd rather not set eyes on me again.'

'I'm sorry if I was rude.' She bit her lip. 'Although Tim wouldn't have noticed anything unusual. He thinks I dislike you.'

James raised an eyebrow. 'And do you?'

She glowered at him. 'As was pretty obvious during the storm I don't any more, otherwise it—that—would never have happened.'

'It happened,' he said deliberately, 'because after spending even a short time with you in Upcote I discovered that Tim's little friend had matured into a woman who appeals to me so much I lost my head that night. But don't worry,

Harriet. As agreed, we just put it behind us, forget it ever happened, and Tim doesn't get hurt.'

Her feelings didn't matter, obviously. 'Right,' said Harriet briskly. 'That's it, then.'

He got up. 'I'll call you a cab.'

She thanked him stiffly, kicking herself for not suggesting it first.

While James was on the phone Harriet stood at one of the windows to gaze at the view, wondering why on earth she felt like crying. 'Thank you for my lunch,' she said politely when he brought her umbrella.

'Thank you for staying to share it. Let me know when you find a new flat and I'll arrange to have your things sent there.'

Harriet's instinct was to insist on paying for her own haulage, but something in his face decided her not to go there. Besides, she needed a favour. 'James, could you possibly store my things in some corner at Edenhurst for a while? I'd like to rent something furnished until I find exactly what I want.'

'Sensible lady.'

'Not always.'

His jaw clenched. 'The fault was mine.'

'It takes two.'

'In your case more sinned against than sinning.'

'We didn't really sin very much.'

His eyes held hers. 'Sins start in the mind, Harriet.'

She smiled bleakly. 'In our case the best place for them.'

When the taxi arrived James escorted Harriet to the lift, pressed the button and stood well back, as though he had no intention of touching her again in this life. 'I'll hold onto your furniture for as long as you want, but I'll let you know the valuation as soon as I get it. Goodbye, Harriet. Take great care of yourself.'

'Goodbye.' Harriet stepped into the lift, feeling as if a

chapter in her life had ended when the doors closed to block James Devereux's face from view.

The following month was a period Harriet looked back on afterwards with wonder that she actually made it to Italy. She had no contact with James other than communications through solicitors, and a letter from some minion with a list of valuations from the Dysart Auction House for the rest of the furniture, along with a cheque for the items James had bought. Harriet paid the cheque into her bank during a lunch hour, wrote a brief letter of thanks on her computer and heard nothing more from James Edward Devereux.

Her usual source of information on the subject was unavailable because Harriet had to warn Tim to stay well away for a while, due to the streaming cold she woke up with the day after her lunch with James. And with no hope of time off straight on top of a week's holiday she was forced to soldier on at work. Giles Kemble had never been ill in his life, and had no qualms about risking Harriet's germs. In an effort to avoid passing them on to Dido, Harriet went to bed the minute she got back to Bayswater every night, and persuaded her friend to go out as much as possible to avoid infection.

After plying the invalid with hot soup and fresh lemonade to wash down a new wonder cold cure she'd found, Dido reluctantly went out with friends, consoled by the fact that Harriet's flat-hunting had to be put on hold for a while. 'I'll miss you terribly when you go,' she said mournfully.

'I'm not exactly emigrating,' said Harriet, coughing. 'We'll see each other just the same.'

'But not so much. I won't see Tim so much, either,' said Dido, refusing to be comforted. 'You look *awful*. I'd better stay.'

Harriet vetoed that firmly. 'You really don't want this cold. In a heatwave it's bad news, believe me.'

Tim rang at regular intervals, as did Alan Green and Paddy Moran, the 'other men' James Devereux had disapproved of so strongly. But there were no phone calls from James, which, she tried hard to convince herself, was a good thing. But when she closed her eyes she could still feel his body against hers, the scent and touch and taste of him. And not for the first time railed against a fate that had landed her in such an impossible situation.

By the end of the week Harriet's cold had improved enough for her to spend social time with Dido. Tim was busy with the French artist whose pictures were about to be shown at the gallery, and he begged for a rain check when offered supper with two females to wait on him hand and foot.

The two females went out on the town instead. When they got back, a little earlier than usual in deference to the convalescent, Harriet was making for bed when Dido suddenly remembered James Devereux's flat.

'You were in bed when I got in that night,' she reminded Harriet. 'Then you went down with your cold, and never said a dicky-bird about the apartment Tim's always banging on about.'

'It's just as amazing as he said, very twenty-first century,' said Harriet, yawning widely.

'You don't sound terribly keen,' commented Dido.

'It's not my kind of thing at all. Everything in the place is white, glass or steel—no carpets, no curtains, and just two blobs of colour on the walls.'

'Are those the paintings Tim talked about?'

'Incessantly.' Harriet chuckled. 'But to be fair they look exactly right. It's no place to hang a Constable.'

'And not your kind of place at all, obviously.' Dido regarded her thoughtfully. 'Funny, really. Tim would move in there tomorrow, given the chance.'

'He won't get it. James is unlikely to vacate his flat just because Tim fancies it.'

'You seem a tad friendlier towards him these days, though,' said Dido.

'It's a move towards better relations between us,' said Harriet firmly.

Dido looked unconvinced. 'Now I've actually met the man in the spectacular flesh I think you'd better take care the relations don't get closer than they should be, my girl. Tim could get hurt.'

Harriet's eyes flashed. 'You know, Dido, you'd be surprised what enormous lengths I go to just to make sure that nothing's allowed to hurt Tim, ever,' she said tartly, and went off to bed.

Flat-hunting was a process Harriet found frustrating. Whenever she found something even remotely suitable Dido, invited on viewings with Tim to keep her in the loop, invariably dismissed it as impossible. But eventually Harriet found a sixth-floor studio flat with City views in Clerkenwell, well within walking distance of the agency where she spent her working day.

Tim helped Harriet with the move, and next day flew off to Italy to stay in the Tuscan farmhouse James had bought years before. Wishing she could have gone with him as planned, Harriet spent the following week putting her new flat to rights in the evenings, and by day worked even harder than usual to make up for her forthcoming absence. And for the first time in their working relationship Giles Kemble astonished her by rewarding her with an early dinner in an expensive restaurant not far from her new flat. Harriet was about to leave the restaurant with Giles when her heart leapt as she saw James arriving with a trio of men. He shot a look at her companion, gave her a frosty, unsmiling nod and, suddenly stricken with acute indigestion, Harriet thanked Giles and trudged home to the flat to pack.

When Dido arrived later she looked unconvinced when Harriet insisted nothing was wrong. She helped with the packing, insisted on staying the night, and next morning even accompanied Harriet on the underground for the journey to Heathrow. When Harriet finally boarded the plane for Pisa later she settled back in her seat with a sigh of pure relief as the plane took off, determined to let nothing spoil the holiday she'd been looking forward to since winter.

When James Devereux had first set eyes on it La Fattoria had been on the verge of crumbling into ruin, but its rose-tinted stone walls and high square tower endeared the ancient farmhouse to him on sight. He went straight ahead with the purchase and immediately began the expensive, painstaking process of restoration, which was slow, due to business commitments that kept him from making all the supervising trips to Italy he would have liked. The restoration was only half finished when he met Madeleine, but her take on an Italian holiday was a five-star hotel in Positano. Whenever James proposed a visit to show her La Fattoria there was always some fashion shoot or social occasion that made it impossible for her to go. And by the time La Fattoria was ready for occupation, complete with swimming pool, the marriage was over and James spent his holidays there with Tim, or with friends, or alone.

Harriet had been invited to accompany Tim there often enough, but this was the first time she'd said yes to a visit to La Fattoria. When she landed in Pisa she was full of anticipation as she boarded the train for Florence, happy to sit gazing, delighted, at the passing scenery until the train drew into Santa Maria Novella station, where she had to wait for a while until another train drew in and Tim, sun-tanned, his hair bleached to ash fairness by the Tuscan sun, alighted from it and raced towards her along the striped marble concourse. After hugs and kisses and apologies for being late, he took charge of the heavier bags and hurried her out of the station.

'We have to walk a bit to get your hire car,' he informed Harriet, 'but it's not too far.'

He was right. But the sun was hot, the picturesque streets of Florence thronged with slow-moving crowds, and by the time they'd taken possession of the car Harriet was only too glad to let Tim take the wheel. Once out of the city he took the scenic route, which wound past the famous wine estates of Chianti. But eventually Tim turned off on a nar-rower road which, he said, with pride in his increasingly fluent Italian, was one of the *strade vicinali*, the local roads that meandered, sometimes aimlessly, all over the Italian countryside.

'But this one leads straight to La Fattoria because the place was a working farm back in the mists of time—not that you can call this straight, exactly,' he added as the car ascended in swooping curves lined with pointing fingers of cypress. Harriet already knew the house by sight from the countless photographs Tim had taken to show her, but when he drove through an archway in the restored outer wall her first actual sight of La Fattoria took her breath away. Green creeper wreathed part of the lower walls, but the square stone tower looking down on the courtyard glowed cinna-mon and gold in the afternoon sun.

Tim leapt out to open Harriet's door, grinning in delight at her expression. 'Cool, isn't it?'

'Cool!' She gave him a scornful look as she got out. 'It's like something out of a fairy tale.'

'And you're in the tower room, princess, for the best view. We'll stow your gear, then have a swim.'

Unlike James Devereux's London flat, the interior of La Fattoria matched the outside, with a high-beamed ceiling, glowing rugs on the cool tiled floor, and supremely comfortable, dateless furniture.

'Jed's got great taste,' said Tim with pride.

'It's lovely,' said Harriet, so quietly he shot her a searching glance.

'You're disappointed?'

'Of course not. How could I be? It's perfect.' She smiled at him. 'But I need a shower and a drink of some kind, and then that swim.'

A winding stone staircase led up to the room in the tower. The bed was wide, with crisp white covers and a headboard carved from the dark wood of the settle beneath the window, and an armoire not unlike the one at End House. Filmy curtains stirred languidly at windows that looked down on the courtyard, and beyond to a blue swimming pool set in a terrace with breathtaking views of olive groves and vineyards against a backdrop of rolling, wooded hills. Harriet gazed out in rapturous silence for a moment before smiling at Tim.

'For once, Tim Devereux,' she said, kissing him, 'you were not exaggerating. But, to make my day complete, does that door lead to a bathroom?'

After a good night's sleep to get over her flight, Harriet was happy to fall in with Tim's plan of as much exploration of local Tuscany as possible. With his encouragement she climbed all five hundred and five steps to the top of the bell tower alongside the Palazzo Pubblico in Siena to look down on the great fan-shaped square, and the view of what appeared to be all of Tuscany beyond. But in Florence next day, after hours of standing in line to see the paintings in the Uffizi and the Pitti Palace, she rebelled.

'That's it. I saw Michelangelo's David years ago when I came here with my school, thank God, so if you can't leave here without looking at him again for the umpteenth time I'm going shopping. I've overdosed on culture, Timothy Devereux. No more pictures, no more *duomos*. From now on I just want to chill.'

The caretakers James employed were away on their annual holiday, but their married daughter came in from the village for an hour or two each morning to tidy up, and bring fresh bread and vegetables. Lunch each day consisted of melon with Parma ham, or a simple salad of tomatoes with basil and mozzarella. Afterwards there were short, leisurely explorations of the countryside in the car, and in the evenings a simple pasta dinner in the courtyard. It was a relaxing, unwinding routine Harriet enjoyed to the full until a little after midnight halfway through her holiday.

Surprisingly tired after a day of doing very little at all, Harriet had been deeply asleep until something disturbed her. She stirred, surfaced slowly and opened her eyes to see James standing in a shaft of moonlight at the end of the bed. She smiled at him drowsily for a moment, and then shot upright in shock. It was no dream. He was here, in the flesh.

'I frightened you,' said James tersely. 'I'm sorry, Harriet. I didn't expect to find you here.'

She pulled the sheet up over the heart banging against her ribs. 'But you knew I was coming to La Fattoria.'

'I meant here in my room.'

'Oh.' She heaved in a shaky breath. 'I didn't know it was your room. Tim didn't tell me.'

He cast a glance at the bathroom door. 'Where is Tim?'

Too tired and dazed to think up some story, Harriet told him the truth. 'He's in Florence.'

'What the hell is he doing there?' demanded James, in a tone that made her want to duck under the covers and hide.

'He's meeting an artist he thinks Jeremy might exhibit at the gallery.'

'Why didn't he take you with him?'

'I preferred to stay here.'

'When did he go?'

'A few days ago,' she said reluctantly.

'A few *days* ago!' James stared at her in furious disbelief. 'And when, exactly, is Tim coming back?'

'I'm not sure. He'll ring me tomorrow.'

His eyes glittered angrily. 'Are you telling me that he left you alone here, miles from anywhere in a strange country, and you have no idea when he'll be back?'

She stared at him mutinously. 'I've got the hire car and my phone, and this place is so idyllic I'm perfectly happy on my own.'

James took in a deep breath, very obviously fighting to control his temper. 'Go back to sleep,' he said brusquely. 'We'll talk in the morning.'

Harriet slumped back on the pillows when the door closed behind him, her heart still thumping from the shock of finding a man in her room. Only it wasn't just a man, it was James. And it wasn't her room, either. It was the master bedroom, and the master had not been at all pleased to find it occupied.

She slid out of bed, and then snatched at her dressing gown as the door flew open and James strode in again.

'Some of Tim's belongings are in his room. And not from the last time he stayed, either. Have you two fallen out?'

'No.'

'Then why are you in separate rooms?'

'I refuse to answer such a personal question,' she snapped, taking the war into the enemy's camp.

'I insist that you do, Harriet,' he rapped at her.

'I won't.' She shook back her hair defiantly. 'If you want answers, ask Tim.'

'I want them from you. If Tim's done something to upset you, I want to know.'

'He's done nothing at all to upset me!'

James eyed her grimly. 'He invites you here for a holiday, then takes off and leaves you alone in a place as remote as this, and you call it *nothing*?'

'I've been fine,' she snapped. 'At least I was until I woke up to find a man in my room.'

'I've explained the reason for that,' he said curtly.

'But not why you're here at La Fattoria,' Harriet reminded him. 'Tim didn't say you were coming.'

'He didn't know.' He paused, as though choosing his words. 'I spent the weekend in Umbria at the Mayhews' villa, but this evening I decided to leave a day early and call in here before my flight back tomorrow.'

'Quite a surprise!'

'Obviously not a pleasant one,' he said, moving nearer.

Harriet backed away. 'Men don't normally appear in my room in the middle of the night.'

'So you keep telling me.' He took her hands. 'I want the truth, Harriet. Has Tim hurt you in any way?'

'That's a change,' she said scornfully. 'Normally I'm the one accused of hurting Tim.'

His eyes locked on hers. 'I keep thinking of something you said at End House, that Tim always goes his own sweet way. Does that mean regardless of your feelings in this instance, Harriet?'

She shook her head. 'Tim would never deliberately hurt me, James.'

'That doesn't answer my question.' His grasp tightened. 'Did you know about the stay in Florence before you arrived here?'

'No more questions, James.'

His face was expressionless in the moonlight. 'Just one. Who was he?'

She frowned. 'Who do you mean?'

His grasp tightened painfully. 'You know damn well! The man I saw you with last week.'

She glared at him, and wrenched her hands away. 'It was Giles Kemble, the man I work for.'

'And do you enjoy regular cosy dinners with your boss?'

'Not that it's any business of yours, but that was the first. I'd worked overtime the entire week, and it was his way of showing appreciation.'

'A damn sight too much appreciation from where I was standing.' James recaptured her hands, a glitter in his eyes that rang alarm bells in her head. 'For a split second when you first woke up tonight you looked utterly delighted to see me. Were you?'

Harriet bit her lip. 'That's not fair.'

'Were you?' he persisted, drawing her closer.

'Yes,' she said gruffly. 'But I thought I was dreaming.'

'This is no dream. We're both flesh and blood, and God help me, I want you so much I'm going insane,' he said, in a tone that made her tremble.

The moonlight cast such a dreamlike quality over the shadowy tower room Harriet's will to resist was almost non-existent even before James drew her close. When she breathed in the scent of warm, aroused male Harriet's last defences crumbled, and sensing it he held her close against him, pressing kisses all over her face. By the time his mouth settled on hers they were on fire for each other and he kissed her until her head reeled, his lips and tongue so demanding that hot, unadulterated need short-circuited something in Harriet's brain. She helped instead of hindering when he ripped her nightgown away, and surrendered to the rapture of his skilled, unerring hands as they sought secret places that reacted with such wanton delight her knees gave way when his mouth streaked down her throat to graze on erect, quivering nipples. She gave a husky little moan, and James pushed her down on the bed and plunged his fingers into tight wet heat, rendering her mindless before he surged between her thighs, his mouth on her throat as they came together in such perfect rhythm it rushed them all too quickly to a climax that overpowered them and left them staring, dazed and breathless, into each other's eyes.

Harriet was first to recover as she scrambled away to hunt out her dressing gown. No point in looking for the nightgown he'd torn from her. A great shiver ran through her as she yanked the sash of her robe round her and tied it viciously tight. She made for the bathroom and stood under the shower, holding her face up blindly to the beat of the water as long as she could bear it, then wrapped a towel round her wet hair, shrugged into her dressing gown, and ventured a look at herself in the mirror. Face flushed, mouth a little swollen, a few tell-tale red marks on her throat, but otherwise she looked much the same as usual. Harriet collected a hairbrush, and went into the bedroom to find James standing motionless at the open window. He'd pulled on his jeans but his chest was bare. He was staring down at the moon's reflection in the pool, so still he could have been one of the marble statues Tim had taken her to see at the Bargello in Florence.

He turned to her, his face in shadow as he stood with his back to the moonlight. 'I don't know what the deal is with you two, but I wish to God Tim had been here.'

Oh, right. Not, Thank you, Harriet, for some terrific sex, then. She said nothing, switched on the lamp beside the bed, sat down on the edge and removed the towel to rub at her hair.

James sat down beside her, staring at his bare feet. They were good feet, thought Harriet, long and slim with straight toes. Not a male feature she'd ever thought of as attractive before—or thought of at all.

'What are you thinking?' he asked.

'That you have rather nice feet.'

He gave a choked sound that was almost a laugh. 'No one's ever told me that before.'

'I thought someone with your looks would be used to compliments.' She took up the hairbrush, looking at him searchingly as she drew it through her hair. 'You obviously regret what happened just now.'

'How could I? That was the nearest thing to perfection two people can achieve together.' He cleared his throat, sounding more like an awkward teenager than the supremely self-confident man she was used to. 'After I saw you with that man the other day I couldn't get you out of my head. I was jealous, for God's sake. I know I don't have a right to be. I accepted the invitation to the Mayhews' just to have an excuse for coming here. It was no impulse visit on the way back. I needed to see you. Though God knows this wasn't my intention. I had no idea Tim was missing. But when I found you were alone here I lost it so completely I never even gave a thought to protection.'

'I take the pill,' she said wearily, 'so you don't need to beat yourself up about that, at least. For the rest we just add this to the list of things we keep from Tim.'

'You don't intend telling him, then?'

'No. My relationship with Tim is a pretty hardy plant. It would survive if it were any other man. But because it's you I won't take the chance.'

'Thank you. Tim would forgive you anything, but if he knew about this he'd never forgive *me*.' James got up, stood looking down at her for a moment, then said goodnight and left her alone.

Not even a goodnight kiss, she thought bitterly.

*   *   *

When Harriet woke next morning full recall of the night swamped her for a moment. She shivered, and went to the window to see James powering along the pool as if he had demons after him. She washed and dressed hurriedly, thrust her feet into flip-flops and raced down the winding stairs at breakneck speed to arrive in the kitchen just before Anna came in with her laden basket. With the usual mixture of phrase-book Italian and hand-waving Harriet managed to inform her that there were two for breakfast.

Anna beamed, assuming Tim had come back, but visibly sprang to attention when Harriet informed her that it was Signor Devereux this time. In minutes coffee was scenting the air, rolls were heating in the oven, and the table ready with several kinds of preserves and a pitcher of freshly squeezed orange juice. When James came in, damp about the head, Anna smiled in shy delight as he thanked her in fluent Italian.

'So you're a linguist, too,' said Harriet as the girl went off to do the household chores.

'I had to learn Italian fast when I first bought this place,' he said, taking the chair opposite. He looked at her closely. 'How are you this morning, Harriet?'

'Tired,' she said, and poured juice for him. 'I didn't sleep much. I wasn't looking forward to facing you this morning.'

'Why?' James buttered a roll and passed it to her, a small service she found oddly touching.

Hormones out of kilter, she told herself, which was no surprise after the events of the night. 'You know exactly why, James Devereux. Last night—'

'We need to do some very serious talking about last night,' he interrupted, and frowned as her phone rang. 'If that's Tim don't tell him I'm here.'

She checked the caller ID, nodding at James in confirmation. 'Hi, Tim.'

'Hi, gorgeous. Are you all right?'

'Yes.'

'That's my girl. I'll be with you sometime this evening. So what have you been doing?'

'Swimming, sunbathing, nothing much,' said Harriet, colouring as she met the eyes fixed on her face. 'See you later, then.'

'If you blush like that when Tim arrives,' remarked James as he poured coffee, 'he can't fail to know something's wrong.'

'No more than he'd expect. Tim will take it for granted I'm not happy about having a visitor.'

'You mean this particular visitor.'

'Exactly.' Harriet frowned. 'But if Tim's not coming until tonight you won't see him before you leave.'

'I've postponed my flight. I need a serious talk with my little brother,' said James grimly. 'You'll have to put up with my company for another night.'

'There's a whole day to get through before then.'

'You don't have to spend it with me. I can take myself off somewhere and come back later. But first we talk. Come out and sit by the pool.'

For the past few days Harriet had enjoyed reclining under a canopy on one of the cushioned steamer chairs, with a cold drink, a radio-cassette player, a pile of books on the table beside her and the occasional swim in the pool to cool her down. Determined not to let James spoil her routine, she stripped down to the bikini under her halter and shorts, smoothed on sunblock, put on dark glasses and stretched out on one of the chairs.

'So what shall we talk about?' she asked.

James tore his eyes away from the expanse of sun-gilded skin and took the other chair. 'I want some answers, Harriet. I've done a lot of thinking since we met in Upcote.'

'About what?'

'Tim.'

Harriet controlled herself with difficulty. 'Don't you ever think about anything, or anyone, else?'

'God, yes. I think about you a damned sight too much. Which is why I turned up here last night. I drove miles out of my way to see *you*, not Tim.' He turned to look at her. 'I was jealous of the man I saw you with that day, but here comes the real joke. I'm also jealous of my own brother. And because Tim thinks the world of you, Harriet, I can't do a damned thing about it.'

'I'm not a pound of tea! Don't I have something to say on the subject?' she demanded.

James nodded impatiently. 'Of course you do, which is where the questions come in.' He was silent for a while, but at last he swung his feet to the ground and sat on the footrest of his chair. 'Last night I found that you and Tim are not sharing a room here. Take those glasses off,' he added. 'I can't talk to a mask.'

With reluctance Harriet put them on the table beside her.

'And living together is not an option, you told me, until after the wedding. So tell me the truth, Harriet. After last night I've a right to know. Are you and Tim no longer lovers?'

She was silent for a while, tempted to lie through her teeth, but at last gave it up. Enough was enough. 'Tim and I have never been lovers,' she said flatly, and met his astounded eyes head-on. 'We're not just good friends, either. It's a much closer relationship than that. I suppose to me he's the brother I never had,' she added, watching James' body relax, muscle by muscle, before her eyes.

'And do you feel like Tim's sister?' he said guardedly.

Harriet grinned. 'More like his mother sometimes.'

He pounced, eyes gleaming. 'So tell me, little mother. What is Tim really doing in Florence?'

This time Harriet had a well-rehearsed answer ready.

'He's practising his powers of persuasion on an artist he wants to come to London.'

His eyes narrowed. 'Why don't I believe you?'

She lifted a bare shoulder. 'I'm telling the truth, James.'

'I still think there's something you're keeping from me.' He seized one of her hands. 'So here's the question I wouldn't ask another soul, Harriet. To my knowledge Tim's never had a close relationship with any woman but you. So if you and Tim are not lovers, is there something else I should know?'

'What are you asking?'

'You know damn well. I'm asking if Tim's gay.'

She gave him a long, hard look. 'Would it make any difference to you?'

'None,' he said, with such utter conviction she believed him. 'Tim is Tim. Now I know he's not your lover, Harriet, I can cope if he's gay.' He smiled at her crookedly. 'But if he's involved with Jeremy Blyth I don't want to know.'

'He's not,' Harriet assured him, chuckling. 'Jeremy is his employer, pure and simple.'

'There's nothing pure or simple about Jeremy Blyth!'

'I wouldn't know about that.' She looked at James steadily. 'And Tim's sexual preferences are not something I'm prepared to discuss. You'll have to ask him yourself.'

'I can't do that!'

'Then forget about it. Take Tim as he is, warts and all. In my book that's what loving someone means.'

'You're right,' James said slowly, and gave her a slow, transforming smile that melted her bones. 'Do you have any idea how good I feel right now?'

'Even without your questions answered?'

'You gave me the answer I wanted most. If you're not Tim's lover there's nothing to stop you from being mine,' he said, with such casual certainty Harriet felt her hackles rise.

'Only my own choice,' she pointed out.

'You had a choice last night.' He leaned forward urgently. 'As far as I'm concerned you made it.'

'And soon regretted it.'

James shot upright. 'I disappointed you?'

'Yes,' she said, pleased when she saw colour flare in his face. 'Afterwards, not during,' she added kindly. 'The sex was utterly wonderful. But your attitude later rather took the shine off it.'

He scowled. 'Surely you understood? I felt guilty as hell because I'd just made love to my brother's future wife.'

Harriet glared back. 'If I had been I wouldn't have let you near me.'

'But you did,' he said swiftly. 'Why?'

'For obvious reasons.'

'They're not obvious to me.'

Her chin lifted. 'I'd spent several days alone in the most romantic setting anyone could ask for, and suddenly there you were in my moonlit tower room, the perfect answer to a maiden's prayer.'

'So I might not have been so lucky on a wet night in Clerkenwell,' he said, in a tone that brought colour to her face.

'You've heard about my move, then,' said Harriet, and retaliated by stretching like a cat, her hands clasped behind her head in a way that threatened the security of her bikini.

James flung away, swallowing, to stare at the pool. 'Tim told me before he left. Not the exact address,' he added. 'So let me have it before I go.'

Right between the eyes if he asked like that, thought Harriet resentfully, and sat up to put on her shirt. 'I must go and find Anna. She's brought food for supper tonight, but I assume you'll be here for breakfast tomorrow. I'd better put in an order for more supplies.'

'What do you normally do for lunch?' said James, getting to his feet.

'I eat tomatoes and mozzarella, mainly, and in the evening I throw pasta in a pot and heat whatever sauce Anna has brought for me. I told her yesterday that Tim might be back tonight, so she's brought extra today.' Harriet smiled magnanimously. 'You can share both meals, if you like.'

'I'd rather take you out to dinner.'

'No, thanks. We'd better be here for Tim.'

'Then I accept your offer. With the greatest of pleasure,' James added deliberately.

In the kitchen Anna smiled shyly and indicated a large round tin containing a hazelnut torte and told them about the pudding she'd put ready in the refrigerator, as well as the usual pan of fragrant sauce waiting on the stove.

Harriet thanked her warmly and gave her a list of provisions needed for next day. 'Anna's husband brings her each morning, but I drive her home,' she told James. 'You can do that today.'

While they were gone Harriet went upstairs, chuckling when she looked into Tim's room. The bed had been made up with fresh linen, and Tim's belongings moved to the smaller room next door. If the master couldn't sleep in the master bedroom, Anna obviously felt he should at least have the larger of the two guest rooms.

The tower room was so immaculate Harriet was almost convinced that the bliss she'd experienced there in the night was imaginary. But at the mere thought of it inner muscles tightened and her pulse raced, confirming it had been all too real. And utterly wonderful. She sighed as she looked at her tanned, glowing reflection. Before it could happen again James had to forget any hang-ups from the past and see her as a person in her own right, not as part of a team with Tim.

Harriet swapped her bikini for shorts and yellow halter,

and went back downstairs to find that the house felt empty without James. She shook her head in derision. She'd been on her own for days, other than the early mornings when Anna was there. Yet James had been here only a few hours and already she felt lonely without him. She tried hard to concentrate on her book, but it seemed like hours before he returned to find her in her usual place by the pool, reading under the canopy. She looked up with a smile as he strolled towards her.

'You've been a long time.'

'People know me now in the village. I stopped to chat, and did some shopping.' He frowned as he noticed her clothes. 'Why did you change?'

'I dressed for lunch,' she said, getting up. 'Do you want it out here or indoors?'

'In the kitchen,' he said promptly, and held out his hand. 'Come inside, it's too hot for you out here.'

When they reached the kitchen Harriet discovered why James had insisted on eating indoors. The kitchen table wore a fresh cloth laid with wineglasses and silverware and the blue ceramic pot of pink geraniums Anna had put there at breakfast time. A central platter held creamy slices of mozzarella and red, juicy tomatoes, rolls steamed invitingly in a basket, and Harriet gave James a smile so radiant he bent to plant a swift kiss on her mouth.

'I deserve that,' he informed her.

'You certainly do. This is lovely.'

'But not difficult. You gave me the menu, and the ingredients were to hand. I put this in to chill before I drove Anna home.' He took a bottle of prosecco from the fridge and filled their glasses. 'And,' he added smugly, 'I tore basil and drizzled oil over the tomatoes in true Michelin-star fashion.'

Harriet sat in the chair he pulled out for her, very much aware that things had changed between them. Now James knew the truth about her relationship with Tim his attitude towards her was different, that of a man on equal footing with a woman he found attractive in the normal way of things, rather than a man trying to resist forbidden fruit. When she told him this, his eyes lit with a gleam that sent a shiver down her spine.

'Perceptive creature. Those were my exact feelings when I found that the schoolgirl had suddenly changed into a woman.'

'I didn't "suddenly change" into anything,' she said tartly, helping herself from the platter. 'The process happened in the usual way. You just didn't notice.'

'I didn't see enough of you to notice once you went off to college. When I was in Upcote it was a rare occasion that you came anywhere near me with Tim.' James tore a roll in half with sudden force. 'Then not so long ago I went to see an Ibsen play at the National and saw you with some man in the bar in the interval.'

'I noticed you.' Harriet smiled. 'I was with Paddy Moran. He's very keen on Ibsen. Personally I find him a tad gloomy—'

'Don't change the subject.' James gave her a wry look. 'It took me a minute or two to realise who you were.'

She smiled provocatively. 'Probably because I was wearing one of my swan outfits.'

'If you mention ugly ducklings again I'll turn you over my knee,' he said forcibly.

Her eyes danced. 'Is that a threat or a promise, James?'

'Both—stop trying to divert me.' He took in a deep breath. 'I saw you with this man and felt angry on Tim's behalf, then not long afterwards I saw you coming out of a cinema with a different man.'

'Did you? I didn't notice you that time,' said Harriet, surprised.

'I was in a taxi waiting for the lights.'

'It must have been Alan Green. We both love the buzz of going to the cinema. Tim prefers to hire a video to watch at home.'

'So do I. Then last week I saw you with someone else. And this time I was angry on my own behalf, nothing to do with Tim.' James gave her a savage look. 'But I was with some clients, which meant I couldn't snatch you away from him.'

'Bad for business,' agreed Harriet, secretly thrilled by the idea.

James was quiet for a moment as he went on with his lunch. 'Once I get things sorted out with Tim,' he said eventually, 'you and I could do that kind of thing together.'

'What kind of thing?'

'Theatre, dinner—anything you want.'

Harriet pushed her plate away. 'I'm not ready for a relationship with you.'

His eyes speared hers. 'Why the hell not?'

'Until quite recently you were someone I actively disliked. I admit I feel quite differently now—'

'How *do* you feel?'

Harriet drank some of her wine. 'I like you much better than I ever thought I would. In the past it was a touch of the Dorian Grays, I suppose. You are beyond question the most attractive man I've ever laid eyes on, but because you trampled on my teenage ego I stored this horrible picture of you in my mental attic. It grew uglier and uglier, until my recent stay in Upcote when I discovered that my grandmother had been right about you all along and I was wrong.' She bit her lip. 'It wasn't the only thing I discovered.'

James reached out a hand to take hers. 'Tell me.'

She gave him a crooked little smile. 'You remember the day I scalded myself? When you put your arm round me, my body was delighted even though my brain told it to behave.'

'The feeling was mutual, as you discovered later.' He frowned suddenly and released her hand. 'I felt guilty as hell afterwards, that night of the storm. But *I* had good reason to. You didn't, Harriet. If you and Tim have never been lovers, why did you push me away?'

'You'll have to ask Tim that.'

'You can count on it. I'm going to ask Tim a whole lot of things,' he promised. 'In the meantime you look tired, Harriet. I'll stow this lot in the dishwasher while you take off to the tower room. Sleep if you can.'

How on earth did he expect her to sleep? But when Harriet reached the cool, welcoming room, the prospect of a nap was so inviting she stripped off her clothes, slid into the bed Anna had made up with fresh sheets, and fell instantly asleep. When she woke James was sitting on the edge of the bed.

'You've been up here for more than two hours,' he said quietly. 'I came to see if you were all right.'

Harriet smiled sleepily. 'I'm fine. I was more tired than I thought.'

James took her hand. 'I was tempted to kiss Sleeping Beauty awake.'

She stretched luxuriously. 'She would have liked that.'

His eyes darkened. He leaned over her to thread his hands through her hair, and bent to kiss her, gently at first, but soon with such hunger Harriet's response was openly ardent. She clasped her hands behind his head to hold him even closer, her lips and tongue eager as they answered his. The sheet fell back and James gave a ragged groan when he found she'd slept nude. He leapt to his feet to shed his clothes, then tossed the sheet away and Harriet felt her nipples harden in response to the look that was as tactile as a caress as he gazed at her for a long moment, before

he let himself down beside her and took her into his arms.
He slid a hand down her spine to draw her close against
him, and Harriet's lips parted against his, damp heat pool-
ing low inside her at the feel of his erection hard and ready
against her. His mouth roamed over her damp skin, grazing
on it with lips and tongue and teeth, then lingering on her
nipples long enough to drive her crazy with longing before
moving on down over her waist and the slight swell below
until he reached the apex between her thighs. She shut her
eyes tightly as she felt the brush of his hair on her skin,
followed by a piercing dart of sensation as his seeking
tongue found the little bud waiting for his caress and she
arched, gasping, and he slid back up her body and entered
it all in one movement, and they lay joined and motionless
for a moment. James looked deep into her eyes and began
to move inside her and her body answered his in perfect
rhythm as he took her slowly at first, then gradually faster,
towards the glory that throbbed and burned just out of reach
as she strove with him to find it. She bit back a scream as
the rush of hot release engulfed her at last, and he collapsed
on her, spent and panting, smiling down at her with the all-
conquering, satisfied look of a man who had just given his
woman the ultimate experience of pleasure.

Harriet grinned at the sheer effrontery of the smile, and
he laughed and kissed her, then turned over on his side and
drew her close with her head on his shoulder, and she
sighed and curved against him, her last thought one of faint
surprise because she needed to sleep again.

The room was dimmer and the shadows longer when
Harriet stirred. She tried to free herself from the arm holding her close, but even in sleep James refused to slacken
his grip, and she looked up into the sleeping face, free to
take her time over it. The glossy black hair was wildly
untidy for once, the eyes hidden beneath closed, thickly
lashed lids. Her caressing eyes moved down over the

straight nose to the wide, positive mouth—then she tensed, her heart thudding. Awkwardly, because of the arm holding her tightly against the hard bare chest, she turned her head to find, for the second time in twenty-four hours, a man standing at the foot of the bed.

CHAPTER SIX

Tim Devereux stood transfixed, his eyes blank with disbelief.

Harriet stared back, horrified, and yanked on the arm constraining her. With a mutter of protest James yawned, opened his eyes and shot bolt upright when he saw his brother.

'About time!' he accused. 'What the hell do you mean by going off and leaving Harriet alone here? Anything could have happened.'

'And obviously did,' retorted Tim, and turned accusing eyes on Harriet as she tugged the covers up to her chin. 'You and *Jed*? How the devil did that come about?'

'I'm not saying a word until I'm dressed,' she said, crimson to the roots of her hair.

James slid out of bed to gather up his clothes. 'You could obviously do with a drink, Tim. We'll join you in ten minutes.'

Harriet shook her head. 'Twenty. I want a shower.'

'Right,' said Tim, still shell-shocked. 'See you later.'

When he'd gone James smiled wryly. 'A spectator sport after all.'

Harriet glared at him, for the moment quite unable to see the funny side of the situation. 'Just go, please.'

'Are you that embarrassed?'

'Embarrassed doesn't begin to cover it,' she retorted. 'Will you please go *away*?'

'It's a little late for maidenly modesty,' he pointed out.

'I'm not getting out of this bed until I'm alone,' she said through her teeth.

'I'll be back for you in fifteen minutes.' James bent to ruffle her hair and strolled from the room.

Harriet wrapped her hair in a towel and rushed through the fastest shower of her life. To boost her morale she put on the outrageously sexy underwear Tim had brought her from Paris and the dress worn at Dido's party, needing all the armour she could muster for the forthcoming confrontation. Tim had never been the slightest put out by her friendships with any other men, but finding her in bed with his idolised brother was another thing entirely. She turned from adding final touches to her face in an ancient gilt-framed mirror to see James watching her from the doorway.

'Ready?' he said, and took her in his arms, but she stood tense in his embrace.

'Ridiculous, I know,' she said, 'but I'm nervous. I keep telling myself it's just Tim.'

James shook her gently. 'Nothing could ever change his feelings towards you. I'm the one who should be worrying.'

'Tim idolises you—'

'Probably not any more, now he's discovered my feet of clay. Let's get it over with.'

On the way down the winding stair Harriet tried in vain to think up something to say to Tim, but when James opened the door to the living room her mind went blank. Tim had company. He faced them proudly, his possessive arm round a strikingly beautiful woman with a mass of black curling hair, her dark eyes fixed on James in appeal.

'Francesca?' he said in astonishment.

'*Come stai*, James?' said the woman, because woman she was, Harriet saw with misgiving.

'And this, darling, is Harriet,' said Tim. 'Harry, I want you to meet my fiancée, Francesca Rossi.'

The silence that followed this announcement was deafening.

'Fiancée?' drawled James at last. 'Is this true, Francesca?'

The look on his face filled Harriet with foreboding. Tim had left certain important details out regarding his Francesca—not only her age, but the fact that James obviously knew her. And possibly in the biblical sense as well as the social one, thought Harriet darkly, newly sensitive to such things after the afternoon she'd just spent.

'Yes, James, it is true,' said Francesca, smiling bravely. 'Will you not give us your blessing?'

From the closed, hard look on James' face the possibility of this seemed remote. 'When did this happen?'

'Last week,' said Tim defiantly.

James turned on Harriet, eyes blazing. 'Did you know about this?'

'No, she didn't,' said Tim at once.

'Did you, Harriet?' repeated James, ignoring him.

'I knew about Francesca,' she admitted reluctantly, 'but not about the engagement.'

The woman smiled nervously. 'Do not discuss me as though I was not here, James. Tim and I have known each other for many years. You know that. You introduced us,' she reminded him.

'I remember. Tim was just a kid at the time. And you were a married woman,' he added deliberately.

Francesca gave him an imploring look. 'But you know that Carlo is dead, James. I am *vedova* now.'

'Not a widow for much longer, darling,' said Tim, gazing down at her possessively. 'You'll soon be my wife.'

'Yes, *tesoro*,' she said, patting his cheek with a hand adorned with a large emerald ring.

'By the way, I've persuaded Jeremy to exhibit some of Francesca's paintings,' Tim told the others triumphantly.

Harriet held her breath as the two men stared at each other with animosity new in their relationship. Tim's eyes were hard and defiant as he faced his brother, with no attention to spare, noted Harriet with sudden heat, for the friend who'd gone to such lengths to keep his love affair secret. James, on the other hand, looked like a volcano about to erupt, which made her decide on escape as the most sensible move.

'I'd love to see your work sometime, Francesca,' Harriet said, smiling brightly, 'but forgive me if I rush off right now. I really must do something about dinner.'

Harriet beat a hasty retreat to the peace of the kitchen, enveloped herself in Anna's apron, opened two bottles of red wine and set to work. She looked up with a scowl when Tim came to join her.

'You're angry with me, I suppose,' he said morosely.

'Is it any wonder?' she retorted. 'You might have told me the truth about Francesca.' She filled a large pan with water, put it to heat then turned on him. 'You not only misled me about her age, you forgot to mention that Francesca and your brother knew each other.'

He shrugged, unrepentant. 'That was the reason for the secrecy. I wouldn't have brought her tonight if I'd known James was here. My plan was to marry her first and tell him afterwards when it was too late for him to do anything about it. Why didn't you warn me on the phone?'

'James wanted to talk to you. Besides, you didn't say a word about bringing Francesca.'

'It was supposed to be a surprise for you.'

'It was certainly that,' said Harriet dryly. 'It was to James, too.'

Tim's mouth twisted. 'An unpleasant one at that. I knew he'd disapprove.'

'I can see his point,' said Harriet, lighting the gas under Anna's sauce. 'Marrying a woman so much older than you was hardly likely to meet with his approval.'

Tim gave her a suspicious look. 'Did you know Jed was coming here?'

'Of course I didn't,' she said scornfully. 'It was a shock when he turned up out of the blue, believe me.'

He gave her a significant look. 'Nothing like the shock I got when I found him in bed with you, my girl.'

Harriet reddened, but returned to the attack. 'He obviously doesn't like this at all, Tim. I just hope Francesca doesn't cause a permanent rift between you.'

Tim took a cloth from a drawer and covered the table, his face set in lines new to Harriet. 'You mean he might stop my allowance.'

Her eyes narrowed. 'What allowance?'

'How do you think I pay for my share of the house in Chelsea? My salary isn't exactly astronomical.'

'It seems there are a lot of things I don't know.'

'No need to look down your nose.' Tim gave her a look that brought colour rushing to her face again. 'I found you naked in my brother's arms, remember. You're in no position to disapprove. Neither is he. What did Jed think he was playing at? As far as he knew, you were my property.'

'I'm nobody's property!' Her chin lifted. 'I told James the truth today.'

'So he promptly rushes you off to *bed*? I thought you two disliked each other. God knows you've always behaved as if you did!'

'When I was in Upcote I discovered a few things which changed my mind,' said Harriet. 'He was very kind to my grandmother, for one thing, and to the young couple I told you about. He was kind to me, too.' And unknown to Tim, his brother was the first man in her life to fill her with lust at the mere touch of his hand.

'A damn sight more than kind if he got you into bed with him!' Tim looked suddenly embarrassed. 'As far as I know, you don't normally go in for that kind of thing, do you, Harry?'

'Not lately! How could I when I was supposed to be marrying you sometime soon? At least my social life should improve again now the truth's out about you and Francesca.' She paused, eyeing him unhappily as she steeled herself to speak her mind. 'Look, are you really sure this will work out, Tim? Francesca's beautiful, and I know you have the art side of things in common, but she's years older than you. Lord knows *I* feel like your mother sometimes and I'm only twenty-three.'

For the first time in their relationship Tim gave her a look so coldly hostile her heart contracted. 'Age difference didn't keep you out of my brother's bed, did it? And in case you're worried, my relationship with Francesca has nothing to do with Oedipus,' he added, in a tone she'd never heard from him before. 'Not that it's any business of yours, but after her husband died we became lovers in the full, normal sense of the word. If you don't approve, tough. After all,' he added, twisting the knife deeper, 'it's my brother's approval I need, not yours.'

Harriet stared at him, stricken, then turned away to take pasta from a cupboard. She swallowed hard, keeping her back to Tim while she poured the pasta into boiling water. She added salt and olive oil, took a look at her watch, and turned to face Tim with her feelings under control. 'Dinner will be ready in ten minutes…'

But Tim had already gone, and Harriet was left gazing, devastated, at the door slammed shut behind him.

Dinner parties had never featured much in Harriet's life, and she would have given much not to be part of this one. There was no dining room at La Fattoria, but the kitchen was large enough for a table and six chairs under the window looking out on the courtyard. Gleaming crystal and silverware, and candles in white pottery holders on a red cloth, gave an air of festivity very much at odds with Harriet's frame of mind. When the kitchen door opened she pinned on a smile that died abruptly when James came in with a face like thunder.

'Why the hell didn't you tell me Tim was involved with Francesca Rossi?' he demanded.

'Oh, so I'm to blame again!' said Harriet furiously. 'Tim made me promise *not* to tell you, of course. And now I've met Francesca I can see why. He deliberately gave me the impression that she was too young to marry, not too old. You were her lover at one time, too, I assume?' she added, carrying the war into the enemy's camp.

James glared at her in distaste. 'Certainly not. I met her when I bought La Fattoria from her husband. Carlo Rossi was a wealthy man with influential connections in this part of the world. He was deeply interested in my plans for the restoration here, and put me in touch with the people I needed to get things done.'

'So you know Francesca well, then?' she said, deflated.

'Not as well as I knew Carlo. He was a cultured, erudite man and I was lucky enough to enjoy Rossi hospitality on several occasions.' His eyes glittered coldly. 'Even if I had been attracted to Francesca she was married to a man I liked and respected, therefore doubly off limits as far as I was concerned. Tim obviously doesn't suffer from the same scruples. She was still very much married when I introduced her to him in Florence five years ago.'

Harriet sighed. 'I remember. He came back from Italy with stars in his eyes, saying he'd fallen madly in love.'

'He was a teenager with rampant hormones. It was lust, not love.'

Harriet shrugged. 'Whatever they are, his feelings haven't diminished in any way. And Lord knows he's seen enough of Francesca over the years to know his own mind.'

James' eyes narrowed. 'And how, exactly, has he managed that?'

'She joins him on the trips he takes for Jeremy Blyth, including Paris recently. And when he's supposed to be here on holiday he spends most of the time in Florence with Francesca. He asked me to come this time just so I could meet her.' Harriet eyed him unhappily. 'He really does love her, James.'

His mouth twisted. 'If it's lasted this long I suppose he does. Though God knows what Francesca thinks she's playing at.'

'Maybe she feels the same about him.'

'I doubt that, but forget Francesca for a minute,' he commanded. 'Let's talk about *your* role in all this. I suppose you and Tim thought it was utterly hilarious to con me with your cute little double act. You most of all, Harriet, with your talk about waiting to marry before living together!'

Harriet's chin lifted. 'I was actually quoting Tim, but in some ways I have similar views.'

'Really?' He smiled sardonically. 'If so I doubt you'll find another man to share them.'

Feeling thoroughly fed up with the Devereux brothers by this time, she shrugged indifferently. 'Then I'll live alone for the rest of my life. A prospect,' she added with sudden passion, 'which strongly appeals to me right now. Will you call the others, please?'

The sauce was deliciously piquant, the pasta perfectly al dente and the wine mellow, but a meal with two of the diners trying desperately to keep the conversational ball in the air, and the other pair barely civil to each other, made for a trying evening. Harriet was desperate to escape by the time she'd served Anna's luscious berry pudding. The two glasses of Barolo downed like medicine had done nothing to make the evening more bearable. Instead the wine gave

Harriet a headache which grew worse when Tim brought up the subject of sleeping arrangements.

'Francesca will share with me, of course, so you two can keep to your bed in the tower room. James, I moved your things back out of my room,' he told his brother defiantly. 'Francesca was in such a state of nerves when I told her you'd turned up, I didn't tell her I found you in bed with Harriet.'

Francesca looked from Harriet to James in astonishment. 'You are lovers? But Tim says you don't like each other.'

Harriet smiled sweetly. 'Ah, but it's unnecessary to *like* a man to fancy some sex with him, Francesca.' She put the torte on the table, enjoying the various reactions on the three faces. 'If you want coffee with this, please make some, but forgive me if I say goodnight and leave the rest of you to clear away. Anna made up the bed in the other guest room for you, James,' she added, and walked out with her head in the air.

Harriet's fleeting triumph had given way to deep depression by the time she reached the tower room. She could have wept as she leaned at the open window to breathe in the cool night air. The holiday she'd been looking forward to for so long was utterly ruined. Even if James caught the next available flight back to England, as she fully expected, she hated the very thought of staying on here with the other two.

The night was no more restful than she'd expected it to be. Harriet read determinedly until her eyes grew hot and itchy, but sleep stayed out of reach. She felt utterly miserable as she watched a beam of moonlight creep slowly over the floor. For months she'd played along with the stupid deception, just to keep James in the dark about the real love of Tim's life. Yet now, for the first time in all the years she'd known him, Tim had turned on her in fury, just for daring to voice an opinion about his relationship. She frowned suddenly. Francesca had been wearing a very impressive ring. If Tim's finances had to be augmented by James, where had the money come from for a rock like that?

But it was nothing to do with her any more, James Devereux included. Tears leaked from the corners of her eyes. After the bliss of his lovemaking he'd cut her to pieces with his furious accusations. As though she were to blame, not Tim. But no wonder he was angry. Until recently Francesca Rossi had been the wife of a man James deeply respected and looked on as a friend. This was the pill James found too bitter to swallow, not her age. What a gullible fool I've been, thought Harriet wearily. But good luck to Francesca. She had a young, adoring lover who not only brought romance and travel into her life, but had even arranged a London exhibition of her paintings. What more could a woman ask?

Next morning Anna took over the task of providing breakfast for all the guests. Harriet thanked her gratefully and took herself off to the pool before the others came down, but to her annoyance found James there before her.

'Good morning,' he said formally.

Harriet ignored him, took off her shirt and shorts, applied sunblock and, with sunglasses firmly in place, stretched out to enjoy the early morning sun.

'I've managed to get a cancellation on a flight out of Pisa today,' he informed her.

'Splendid.'

'You're glad to see me go?'

'Euphoric.'

'When do you fly back?'

'Sunday. Thank you so much for allowing me to stay here.' She smiled sardonically. 'It's been *such* a memorable holiday.'

He shot a morose look at her. 'What the hell am I going

to do, Harriet? I can see where Francesca's coming from. She was married to a man old enough to be her father, so of course she likes having a young stud like Tim lusting after her. But that's the problem where he's concerned. He's not thinking with his brain.'

Harriet shrugged. 'What you do about it is entirely up to you. I'm no longer involved.'

He stared incredulously. 'You can't mean that. You're too close to Tim to wash your hands of him entirely.'

'Here's a suggestion.' She took off her sunglasses and turned cold eyes on him. 'Tim is pretty sure you'll cut off his allowance. Francesca might change her mind if you do.'

James shook his head. 'Carlo Rossi was seriously wealthy and she inherited everything. Apparently her work sells well, too, so as far as Tim's concerned money's not her object.'

'Why, exactly, are you so dead against the marriage?' she asked curiously. 'Is it just the age difference or are there a lot more things I don't know?'

He was silent for a moment, his face set. 'I was married to someone older than me,' he said eventually. 'One of the reasons for the breakdown was Madeleine's refusal to have children. The age gap between Francesca and Tim is a hell of a sight bigger than it was in my marriage, so she probably won't want children, either, which Tim is bound to regret one day.'

'I'm a little short on concern for Tim right now,' Harriet said flatly. 'I uttered one little word of caution last night and ten years of friendship went straight down the drain.' She gave James a resentful glare. 'You were quick to put the knife in, too. Frankly, I've had it up to here with both of you. As far as the Devereux brothers are concerned I don't give a damn any more.'

'Where I'm concerned, Harriet, I can well believe it, but not with Tim, surely. You've always been so close. Which brings me to one of the many things that kept me awake last night,' he added, his eyes locking on hers. 'Tell me the truth, Harriet. Was it really just friendship between you and Tim?'

'Yes, it was,' she said stonily. 'So now you can devote all your energies to the problem of Tim and Francesca and forget about me.'

James gave her a long, hard look, as though trying to gauge what was going on in her brain. 'Is that a roundabout way of saying you want nothing more to do with me?'

'Exactly.'

'I see.' He got to his feet. 'It's a longish drive. I'd better get started. Are you all right?' he added, eyeing her closely. 'You ate very little last night.'

'How could I in that atmosphere?' She shuddered. 'I'll just wait to see what Tim's plans are, then take off in the car out of the way. No way am I playing gooseberry to a pair of lovebirds.'

'Stand up, Harriet,' he ordered.

'Why?'

'Just do it.'

As soon as her feet touched the ground James pulled her into his arms and kissed her until her head was reeling.

'A little something to remember me by,' he said roughly. *'Arrivederci!'*

Harriet lay very still for a long time after he'd gone, bitterly regretting the pride that had made her cut off her nose to spite her face, as Livvie used to say. It had forced her to lie to James about not wanting him in her life. Now she had the rest of the week alone to regret it, or maybe not alone if Tim and his *innamorata* were staying until she left.

A miserable hour went by before Tim came strolling round the side of the pool to wish her good morning.

Harriet gave him a frosty nod and went on reading.

'Where's Jed?' he asked.

'He left for Pisa an hour ago.'

'He's keeping to it, then.'

She looked up wearily. 'To what?'

'Opposition to my marriage.' Tim gave her a hopeful smile. 'Could you put in a good word for me when you see him next?'

She stared at him incredulously. 'After the way you turned on me last night? Not a chance!'

'I didn't mean it,' he said, flushing.

'I'm not stupid, Timothy Devereux! You meant every word. Not that it matters. I can't help you with James because I won't be seeing him again.'

Tim's eyebrows shot to his hair. 'You mean that was just a one-off I interrupted yesterday?'

'It's not against the law! Now I'm not playing your stupid game any more I'm free to do that kind of thing as much as I like,' she reminded him. 'Where's Francesca?'

'She's getting ready to face Jed. We thought he was still in bed. I'd better go and tell her he's gone. Then we're going back to Florence. You'll be all right here on your own, will you?' he said, as such an obvious afterthought Harriet almost pushed him in the pool.

'I dare say I'll manage,' she snapped.

'Good,' Tim said absently, all his attention on the woman coming towards them.

Francesca was dressed to impress in an exquisitely plain linen dress, delicate kid sandals and cosmetics applied with a skill Harriet could appreciate from long association with Dido.

'Good morning,' said Harriet politely.

'*Buongiorno,*' said Francesca, and looked nervously at Tim. '*Caro*, where is your brother?'

'On his way to catch a plane to London,' said Tim, kissing her.

'You did not talk to him this morning?'

'No. He left early, darling.'

Francesca looked deeply relieved. 'Then we may leave also.' She turned to Harriet with a warm smile. 'It was so good to meet you at last. Next time you come, you must make a visit to my house and see my paintings.'

After the farewells were over Harriet watched the pair leave, finding their body language very illuminating. Tim was quite right about their relationship, she admitted reluctantly. Francesca Rossi's feelings for her young lover were in no way maternal. His passion was returned in full.

Once she heard the car leave Harriet went indoors to clear up after the late breakfast, waving aside Anna's objections when she came running into the kitchen with an armful of bed linen. Harriet insisted on loading the dishwasher and putting things away, and with much hand waving and smacking of lips complimented Anna on the torte and pudding eaten at dinner the night before. Later, she thought with satisfaction, she could console herself by pigging out on the remains of both in peace.

She was in the courtyard after a solitary dinner that evening when her phone rang.

'I'm back,' said James.

'Oh, hello,' she said coolly, her hostility flaring up again the moment she heard his voice.

'Is Tim there?'

'No. He went back to Florence with Francesca. She seemed relieved that you'd left without saying goodbye.'

'I'm not surprised. I had a pretty blunt talk with her last night. She knows damn well I disapprove.'

'It won't make a scrap of difference. You'll just have to bite the bullet and accept her as a sister-in-law.'

'It worries the hell out of me.'

'It's Tim's life.'

'I know you're right, but it goes against the grain to stand by and let him make a mess of it.' He paused. 'So you're on your own, then, Harriet, just as you wanted.'

'Yes.'

'You don't mind?'

'No. In a beautiful place like this it's sheer bliss.'

'With no more intruders in your bedroom to spoil it.'

'You said it.'

'Harriet, listen to me—'

But she disconnected deliberately, taking petty satisfaction in cutting him off.

Harriet drove back to Florence at the weekend, left the car with the hire firm and took the train to Pisa in pensive mood. There had been no more phone calls from James, but Tim had rung the night before to say he'd wheedled a couple of extra days' holiday out of Jeremy Blyth, and wouldn't be seeing her until he got back to London. He told her to leave the key with Anna, wished her a safe journey home and promised to call in to see her as soon as she got back.

'Don't bother.'

'What?'

'I don't want to see you, Tim. I need some space.'

'You're *that* mad at me?'

'Not mad. Hurt. I need time to lick my wounds.'

'If you ask him nicely, maybe Jed will lick them for you,' he snapped, and rang off.

Harriet sat staring through the train window, seeing very little of the passing scenery on the return journey. She couldn't blame Tim for being crude. Finding her in bed with James would have been a shock to his system. It was still a shock to her own every time she thought of it, which was most of the time. She sighed. She was fed up with Tim right now, but she still cared enough to hope that the affair with Francesca wouldn't end in tears. Harriet shrugged the thought away impatiently. It was high time she concentrated on her own life and stopped mollycoddling Tim Devereux. At least one good thing had come out of it all. James knew beyond doubt that his brother wasn't gay.

CHAPTER SEVEN

HARRIET had dreaded telling her friend that Tim was engaged to someone else, and went straight to Bayswater from Heathrow to get it over with. She did her best to break the news gently, but just as anticipated, Dido was utterly devastated.

'I can't believe it! You two were stringing me along all this time just because Tim's involved with someone older than him?' she said, on the verge of tears.

'It's not like that, Dido. Francesca may be older than Tim, but she's a beautiful woman, and a talented artist. And he's madly in love with her.'

'But you seem so calm about it!'

'It's not a shock to me, love. I've known about Francesca for ages.'

'That's what really hacks me off.' Dido glared at her. 'You could have trusted me, Harriet. Why on earth didn't you *tell* me?'

Harriet sighed. 'I wanted to, believe me, but Tim swore me to secrecy, in case James found out and tried to put a stop to it.'

'Does James disapprove of this Francesca person so much, then?'

'Yes. He knew her first, even introduced Tim to her in the first place.' Harriet pulled a face. 'He regrets that now.'

'Why?'

'Until recently the love of Tim's life had a husband.'

'Good grief,' said Dido, looking sick. 'No wonder James is upset.'

Harriet nodded. 'He's convinced that Tim's heading for

disaster. But I think Francesca's just as mad about Tim as he is about her. And why shouldn't she be? Her husband was much older than her. Tim's young and fun to be with, nice to look at, he loves her to bits and he's probably good in bed, too.'

'*Probably?*' Dido stared, flabbergasted. 'Are you saying you've never found out?'

'Never have, never will. I love Tim, but not in that way.'

'You know that I do,' said Dido forlornly.

Harriet nodded sympathetically. 'But give it up, love. It's never going to happen.'

Dido sighed despondently, and then eyed Harriet in sudden suspicion. 'You seem remarkably clued up about his brother's views on the subject.'

'James made a flying visit to the villa on his way home from Umbria,' said Harriet and diverted her friend by producing the handbag she'd bought for her in Florence.

It was strange to leave later and go on to the flat in Clerkenwell, but Harriet breathed a sigh of relief when she shut her new door behind her at last. She unpacked the clothes Anna had insisted on laundering, made a snack from supplies Dido had bought for her, and when she went to bed later made a conscious effort to put both Devereux brothers from her mind.

By the end of her first, frantically busy working day, Harriet felt she'd never been away. But over supper in the new flat that evening it gradually became clear that she couldn't live with the cobalt blue of the walls. At the weekend paint would be on her shopping list.

When Harriet got home on the Friday evening she found Tim waiting for her, clutching a bunch of flowers.

'I've given you space,' he informed her.

'Not much of it!' She unlocked the entrance door, utterly delighted to see him, but unwilling to let him know how much yet. 'Are those for me?'

'No.' Tim grinned. 'They're the latest accessory for us trendy guys. Jeremy carries a nosegay around with him all the time.'

'I can well believe that,' she said, and shrugged, resigned. 'Oh, all right. Come up, then. When did you get back?'

'This morning.' When they got to the flat Tim put the flowers down and caught her in a hug. 'I'm sorry for the things I said. To you, of all people, Harry. I was completely out of order.'

'You certainly were, you pig. But I had no right to lecture you, either,' she said, her voice muffled against his jacket. Then she looked up. 'Though you should have been straight with me about Francesca.'

'I know,' agreed Tim penitently. 'But if I had, you wouldn't have agreed to the con.'

'You're dead right,' she said with feeling.

'Friends again, then?' he said, his eyes so anxious Harriet smiled affectionately.

'Friends,' she agreed. 'Officially friends now, thank heavens. Masquerading as your significant other had certain drawbacks.'

'Bad for your sex life,' Tim agreed as she arranged the lilies in a vase. 'Talking of which—'

'Let's not, please!'

'If you mean Jed we can't forget he exists.' Tim pulled a face. 'He gave me absolute hell for not taking better care of you.'

Harriet snorted inelegantly. 'He can talk! He gave me hell, too.'

'About Francesca?'

'That, too. But strangely enough I think our cute little double act infuriated him most.'

Tim nodded sagely. 'Nothing strange about it. Jed wants

you bad, my pet. But what's going on? He says you refuse to see him any more.'

Harriet slumped down on the sofa. 'That was my stupid pride talking. I didn't enjoy the row he gave me.' She gave him a wry little smile. 'And between you and me, I didn't care for his high-handed assumption that he could automatically take your place in my life as my, um—'

'Lover? You looked pretty comfortable with the idea when I found you in bed with him,' said Tim slyly, sitting beside her.

She reddened. 'That just sort of happened. Like an avalanche happens. But in normal circumstances I require some creative courtship before letting things get that far with a man, James included.'

'Shall I tell him that?'

Harriet gave him a menacing glare. 'One word and you die!'

'Whatever you say, angel.' Tim smiled at her hopefully. 'I don't suppose you've got any food?'

'Lord, you're predictable. No, I haven't got any food. No time for shopping. Does Francesca know you eat like a horse?'

'Yes. She's got a great cook, thank God.' Tim paused. 'By the way, Harry, Francesca was nervous as hell about meeting you.'

'Really? Why?'

'She's a tad jealous.' Tim smiled fondly. 'She just can't believe that I prefer her to someone young and delicious like you. She says that I'll tire of her, and it won't last.' He sobered. 'But it will. Until death do us part.'

Harriet smiled at him, touched. 'But where on earth did you get the money to buy that ring she was wearing?'

He grinned. 'Are you kidding? It's her mother's. Normally she wears it on the other hand, but I made her swap it over when I found James there.'

'Talking of James, has he stopped your allowance?'

Tim looked sheepish. 'Surprisingly enough, no. I went to see him as soon as I got back, pretty sure he'd cast me off with the proverbial shilling now he knows about Francesca. But he was quite mellow about it, even when I told him I'm going to share her studio after the wedding, and get down to some serious painting at last.'

'Mellow, was he?' Harriet's eyes flashed dangerously. 'So that stupid charade of ours was unnecessary after all.'

'I disagree there.' Tim tapped his nose. 'He was so bloody relieved when he found *you* weren't going to marry me it took the heat right off Francesca.'

She sniffed. 'He's made no effort to contact me since I got back.'

'Are you in love with him?' asked Tim bluntly.

About to deny it hotly, Harriet stared at him, arrested, as the truth hit her between the eyes. The reason for her current lack of joy in life was suddenly obvious. For the first time in her life she was in love. Deeply, desperately in love. And, fool that she was, had demonstrated how much she cared by ordering James out of her life. She groaned in despair. 'Of course I'm in love with him—for all the good it'll do me.'

Tim looked troubled. 'Can't I help things along somehow?'

She shook her head. 'No, thanks. Love unsought is better and all that.'

'Whatever you say.' He gave her a hug. 'Right, then, friend. If you won't let me play Cupid let me feed you instead. Chinese, Indian, or fish and chips?'

Feeling more at peace with the world after making it up with Tim, Harriet went out shopping for paint next morning. She gave in to Dido's pleas to hit the sales with her in the afternoon, but resisted all her friend's coaxing to join her in a spending spree, and went straight back to Clerkenwell afterwards instead of going to a party thrown by one of Dido's friends.

'I must be up bright and early to start painting,' Harriet said firmly.

'Do you have to start right away? Let me treat you to lunch somewhere nice on the river tomorrow instead,' coaxed Dido as they parted at the underground, but Harriet shook her head.

'It's very sweet of you, but I've just got to make a start on those walls.'

Next morning, arrayed in shorts and vest and ancient pink basketball boots, Harriet opened all the windows and moved the furniture to the middle of the room. She pushed her hair up under a baseball cap, veiled the furniture with towels in lieu of dust-sheets, and wrenched her new folding stepladder into position. She filled her new pan with white emulsion, armed her new roller and set to work, but soon found that painting a ceiling took a lot longer than expected because she was obliged to hop on and off the ladder far too often for speed. Wishing vainly that she were taller, with a longer reach, she shifted furniture round from time to time to get better access. Ignoring a crick in her neck, she carried on doggedly, determined not to stop until the ceiling was finished, and only then took time off for a sandwich and a cold drink.

Lunch over, she carried on with the undercoat for the walls, and soon found that the smell of paint had not combined well with her tuna sandwich. She was queasy, sweating, her eyes stinging and her roller arm aching by the time she'd finished the last wall, and said something very rude when the doorbell rang. Dido, she thought, resigned. But when she heard a familiar male voice over the intercom her heart missed a beat, then resumed with a sickening thump.

'May I come up, Harriet?' asked James.

No! Not now, when she was looking such a mess! But instead of banging her head in frustration against her newly painted wall Harriet consented politely and pressed the release button.

When she opened her door to James she stared at him in despair. He was everything she was not. Black hair glossy, olive-skinned jaw newly shaven, casual shirt and khakis immaculate, and above all *clean.* He stood utterly still at the sight of her, his face rigid with the effort to keep it straight.

'I've obviously come at a bad time.'

'You could say that,' she agreed, pretty sure she had a smudge of paint on her nose. 'I can't even ask you to sit down.'

'Could I come in just the same, Harriet? I won't keep you long.'

Without a word she stood aside and motioned him through. 'Wait a moment while I rinse the roller.' She escaped into the tiny cupboard of a kitchen, held the roller under running water until it ran clear, took a despondent look at her paint-splashed face as she washed her hands and decided to stay with the baseball cap rather than struggle with sweat-soaked hair.

'Sorry about that,' she said brightly, returning to James.

'How are you, Harriet?' he asked.

'As you see, busy. What brings you to this neck of the woods?'

'To see you, what else?' He looked at her steadily. 'Tim came round to my place today. He says you've relented towards him.'

She nodded, resigned. 'It's hard to stay angry with Tim for very long, but this time it took a bit longer than usual. I dislike being conned, even by Tim.'

'I felt the same about you,' said James grimly. 'Did you really agree to Tim's idiotic scheme just to make sure I didn't stop his allowance? Am I such a petty tyrant, for God's sake?'

'I knew nothing about the money until that evening at La Fattoria,' snapped Harriet. 'I agreed to the stupid charade because Tim said you disapproved of Francesca. I realise why, now,' she added darkly. 'Tim said it was the age gap, so I took it for granted she was too young for him, not the other way round.'

'Frankly I'm tired of the whole affair. I've taken your advice. From now on Tim can do as he likes, which, as you once tried to tell me, is exactly what he does, anyway.' James shrugged. 'I've no intention of stopping his allowance. He can go and live with Francesca tomorrow as far as I'm concerned.'

'He wants to marry her first.'

'So I gather. Now I've given my blessing I suppose he'll rush her into it as soon as he can.' James paused. 'Tim told me something else today.'

'Oh?'

His eyes took on a gleam Harriet viewed with disquiet. 'He thinks you may also have thawed towards me. Is that true?'

All the answers Harriet thought of stuck in her throat so long James turned to go. 'I dislike the role of mendicant,' he said tersely.

'Don't go!' she said urgently. 'Or better still come back sometime when I'm clean.'

He turned back, the sudden leap of heat in his eyes sending her backing away in alarm. 'You don't want me to touch you?' he said softly, stalking her round the furniture.

'Of course I don't. I'm hot and filthy and I probably smell,' she said despairingly.

His deliberate, relishing sniff sent a wave of scarlet to join the paint streaks on her face. 'You do, Harriet, of your own irresistible blend of pheromones. A pity there's no space to throw you on the floor and ravish you.' He laughed at the shock on her face, and stood back. 'You don't fancy the idea?'

'Not right now, no,' she lied.

'I should have rung first as Tim advised,' he said with regret.

She stared. 'You, taking advice from Tim?'

'On the subject of Harriet Verney he's an expert, he tells me.'

'In his dreams!'

James grinned. 'One thing he said made sense. Subtlety and finesse are vital, according to Tim, if I want to make any headway with you.'

'Tim, preaching subtlety and finesse?' said Harriet, dizzy with euphoria at the mere thought of James wanting to make headway.

'In this case he has a point. So in accordance with his instructions I shall leave you in peace right now, and let you get into that bath you're obviously desperate for, on condition that you have dinner with me tomorrow evening.'

'Sorry, I can't tomorrow, I already have a date.'

'Tuesday then,' said James firmly.

Pride salvaged, she inclined her head graciously. 'Tuesday's good.'

'I'll come for you at eight,' said James.

Harriet closed the door, wishing she had space to dance for joy. Thank you, Tim, she thought gratefully.

When he arrived on the stroke of eight James was wearing a pale, lightweight suit of masterly cut, his slightly darker shirt open at the collar in deference to the hot summer evening, and Harriet could have flung herself into his arms there and then to relieve the tension of getting ready too early in the terracotta linen dress he'd seen twice before.

'Nothing's changed,' said James, looking her up and

down, 'I still feel the urge to throw you on the floor and ravish you, even now you're clean.'

'Not enough space for that,' she said, pulse racing.

'I would have brought you flowers, as Tim instructed,' he informed her as they went down in the lift, 'but it seemed best to wait until you've finishing painting.'

'Sensible,' she approved, and grinned up at him. 'James, I can't believe you're acting on Tim's instructions.'

'Every step of the way,' he assured her earnestly.

To her surprise James took her to the restaurant she'd dined in with Giles Kemble.

'To make up for the last time we ran into each other here,' he said, once they were seated.

Harriet smiled. 'You were so hostile I had indigestion on the way home!'

He reached out a hand to take hers. 'And I invited myself to the Mayhews' place in Umbria the following weekend just so I could call in at La Fattoria to see you again. Doesn't that tell you something, Harriet?'

'What do you mean, exactly?'

James released her hand as a waiter interrupted to pour wine, but once they were alone again he leaned forward, his eyes urgent. 'That night in Tuscany was a revelation. And not just because we made love for the first time, though God knows that was wonderful enough. But learning the truth about you and Tim changed everything. From now on I want you in my life, Harriet.'

James sat back as their first course appeared, and Harriet, still trying to take in what he'd said, stared blankly for a moment at the exquisite arrangement of antipasti in front of her.

To her relief James kept to less emotive subjects during the meal. He asked her about her working day, told her about his own, teased her about her home decorating, and Harriet eventually relaxed, enjoying the evening she'd been looking forward to from the moment he'd left her forty-eight hours before.

'I put the first coat of primrose on last night,' she told him.

He raised a sardonic eyebrow. 'I thought you were going out last night.'

She smiled demurely. 'My date was a pot of paint. To-morrow I roll on another coat, and with a bit of luck that should do.'

'What was the original colour?'

'A murky sort of blue.'

'Not your taste, obviously. Unlike the colour of that dress.' His eyes moved over her bare arms like a caress. 'Did I mention that you look good enough to eat tonight?'

'No, you didn't. Thank you, kind sir. I wore the dress,' she added, 'because the colour reminds me of the flower-pots at La Fattoria.'

'So your memories of the place aren't all unpleasant, then.'

'No.' She looked at him squarely. 'As I said at the time, my holiday there was memorable. My vacations don't nor-mally provide such extraordinary value for money.'

James raised an eyebrow. 'I didn't charge you any money.'

'I know. Thank you.'

'But I think I deserve *something* in return.'

'What would you like?'

'I'll tell you on the way home.'

This, Harriet found, involved a taxi ride to James' home, not a short walk to hers.

'You might have asked me first,' she said as he gave the address to the driver.

He slid an arm round her. 'It's only a little after ten, there's no space to stand up in your flat, let alone sit down, so another hour of your company in comfort at my place is my fee for letting you stay at La Fattoria. Reasonable?'

'I suppose so,' she conceded, secretly thrilled with the idea. Sitting close to him in the taxi, she was filled with delicious anticipation by the scent and warmth of his body. James might not have said so in so many words, but after all his talk of ravishing she had no doubt he was taking her home to bed to make love to her, a prospect that sent her blood racing through her veins.

When they arrived at the familiar redbrick building James paid off the taxi, and held her hand as they went up in the lift to his floor. He unlocked his door, switched off the alarm and pressed a switch to bring a pair of lamps to life alongside the white crescent-shaped sofas. Certain she would be swept into a passionate embrace the moment they were through the door, Harriet was rather taken aback when James led her to one of the sofas instead.

'Sit down, Harriet, and I'll make some coffee, or would you prefer wine?'

She regrouped hurriedly. 'Tea, perhaps?' she said, crestfallen.

James switched on spotlights in the kitchen area, slung his jacket over a chair and made two mugs of tea he carried over on a tray that had been laid ready, and even included a container of biscuits. 'You didn't eat enough dinner,' he commented. 'Do you take milk in your tea?'

'Yes, please,' said Harriet, thoroughly deflated. Tea and biscuits seemed an unlikely overture to red-hot sex on that great bed of his in the other room.

'Have a biscuit,' he ordered. 'You've lost weight.'

'Paint is quite an appetite depressant.' Harriet nibbled obediently on a biscuit. It was easier than arguing.

'When Tim marries Francesca, will you go to the wedding?' James asked.

She shook her head. 'Probably not.'

'Why?'

It was hard to tell a man of James' financial situation that she couldn't afford another trip to Italy. One of the great benefits of the holiday at La Fattoria had been that it came free. All she'd had to do was save up for her flight. Tim had paid for the food she ate there, by way of appreciation for her help with his romance. But in Florence she'd bought a handbag for Dido, and pretty coin purses for her friends at the office. James' cheque for the furniture had gone on the deposit on the new flat, and a few basic necessities for it, but now, after the outlay on home decorating equipment, her finances were at an all-time low.

James turned to look closely at her. 'You're taking a long time to answer.'

'If I get an invitation—'

'Of *course* you'll get an invitation. Tim will probably want you to be bridesmaid at the very least!'

Harriet pulled a face. 'Francesca won't want that.'

'Why not?'

'She's jealous of me, according to Tim. Only because of my age,' she added.

'I can think of other reasons,' said James dryly.

Harriet braced herself. 'Without sounding horribly mercenary, could I ask how soon I can expect the money for End House?'

'Any time now, I should imagine.' He gave her a searching look. 'Are you saying that without it you can't afford a trip to Florence?'

'Yes,' she said baldly.

'For God's sake, Harriet, I'll pay for your flight and anything else you need, including a new dress—'

'No, thanks,' she said quickly. 'I can't let you do that.'

'Why the hell not?'

'Pride,' she said simply.

James leaned nearer and took her hand. 'So you let me have End House because you really needed the money?'

She nodded unhappily. 'I just have what I earn. Livvie didn't have much cash to leave. She'd used most of her capital on my education.'

'So why did you turn me down when I first asked you to sell me the house?'

'Two reasons. One because it was you,' she said bluntly. 'At the time you were my least favourite person, if you recall.'

'Vividly!'

'And secondly I just couldn't bear to part with it. When my parents died my grandmother sold the big London house we'd all lived in together and took me to live in Upcote where she grew up. From the time I was thirteen years old End House was my home.' Her eyes shadowed. 'But now Livvie's gone it's not the same. Without her I don't belong there any more. So in the end I sold it to you.'

James was quiet for a moment. 'If the money means so much to you, Harriet, why did you move out of your friend's flat?'

'The rent on the new one is less than my share of Dido's mortgage, and I can walk to work now, so financially I'm better off. And Dido won't see so much of Tim, too, which is all to the good, because she's in love with him,' explained Harriet.

'Good God, how does he do it?' said James in amazement. 'Does every woman he meets fall for him?'

She laughed. 'It's a trait worth thousands to Jeremy Blyth. When a woman comes to look round at the gallery Tim invariably makes a sale.'

'Tim told you that?'

'No, Jeremy did. Interestingly enough,' added Harriet, 'Jeremy was never taken in for a moment about Tim and me. He told Tim I was the wrong wife for him.'

'Probably wants to marry Tim himself,' said James acidly. 'But he was right about you.'

Harriet got up to put her mug on the tray. 'Time I was going, James.'

'Why not stay here tonight?' he said, and took her hand to lead her past the kitchen and dining area towards what Harriet had assumed to be a blank wall. 'I didn't show you this last time.' He touched a discreet button and a section of wall slid back to reveal another bedroom. 'This is where Tim sleeps when he stays here. A bathroom's concealed behind that glass panel, and on this side you get another view of the Thames.'

Harriet smiled politely to mask her fierce disappointment. Instead of sharing a bed with James a night in the spare room appeared to be the only thing on offer. 'Very nice, but I'd better get back.'

'Sure?' he said gently.

'Positive. Will you ring for a cab, please?'

James made the phone call, and turned to take her in his arms. 'Harriet, what's wrong?'

'Nothing.' She smiled up at him. 'Thank you for dinner.'

'Will you tell me something?'

'If I can.'

'Are you in pressing need of this money?'

She stiffened. 'Why?'

'I just want you to know you can come to me if you have a problem. Of any kind,' he added with emphasis.

'James, I'm fine, honestly,' she assured him. 'I want the money as an investment to give me the security of an additional monthly income to add to my salary. Which is quite respectable, by the way, so you really don't have to worry about me.'

'I'll try not to make a career of it. But I suppose this means you won't take up my offer on Florence,' he said, resigned.

'I appreciate it, but no, thanks—and there's the doorbell. My taxi's here.'

This time James went down in the lift with Harriet, and the moment the doors closed on them he swept her into his arms at last, his mouth on hers in a kiss that lasted until they reached ground level. He smiled into her startled eyes as he raised his head. 'If I'd done that upstairs I couldn't have stopped. And you're obviously not ready for that yet.'

How wrong could a man be? thought Harriet irritably as James handed her into the waiting taxi.

'I'll ring you,' he said, and bent to kiss her again before handing a banknote to the driver.

Her phone rang five minutes after she got in.

'You're home, then,' said James.

'Is this what you meant when you said you'd ring me?' she asked, laughing.

'Yes. It may have slipped your mind, but I made certain overtures about the future before dinner. I want a response, Harriet Verney. Do you like the idea?'

'Yes, James. I do. I like it a lot.' Harriet wished he'd mentioned it again at the flat so she could have shown him exactly how much she liked it.

'Thank God for that! I'll see you on Friday.'

'Are we meeting on Friday?'

'Of course we are. Only this time you stay over and we spend Saturday and Sunday together to give your walls a chance to dry out.'

Harriet blinked. 'I thought you were proceeding step by step, like Tim said.'

'I am. But I'm taking them two at a time.'

CHAPTER EIGHT

BY SEVEN on Friday evening Harriet had changed her clothes twice and repacked her weekend bag more than once, wishing she had some idea of what James had in mind so she could have chosen her weekend gear accordingly. They'd talked on the phone twice, but last night she had been out when he left a message, and when she rang him back she'd had to do the same. And now she was at a fever pitch of anticipation.

This excitement over a man was new in her life. Except for one brief, disastrous encounter, her relationships with men other than Tim had been relaxed, undemanding affairs. With James it was different. Dido was madly in love half the time, and for the duration of each affair became blind to all faults in the man in question. Harriet saw James very clearly, but had no doubt at all that she was in love with him. And would probably stay that way for the rest of her natural life.

She had been waiting for half an hour that seemed twice as long as that by the time her doorbell rang. She snatched up the receiver to hear James' voice and moments later he was at her door, smiling as he handed her a white hydrangea in a yellow porcelain pot.

'Step two,' he said, looking so smug Harriet couldn't help laughing.

'Why, thank you, James,' she said, batting her eyelashes as she took it from him. 'What a lovely surprise.'

He looked round in approval. 'This looks a lot better than on my last visit. You've worked hard. Do you intend painting your bedroom as well?'

Harriet smiled at him pityingly. 'This is my bedroom. It's a studio flat, which is a posh name for a bedsitter. The sofa turns into a bed at night, and the kitchen and bathroom are shoe-horned into a sliver of space behind those doors over there. But it's very convenient for my job, and now my walls are sunnier I think it looks rather good.' She put the plant down on a small wicker table between the two windows, and stood back to admire the effect.

James moved close behind her, sliding his arms round her waist. 'You're supposed to kiss people who give you presents,' he reminded her, his breath warm against her neck.

Harriet twisted round, and reached up to put her arms round his neck. 'So I've heard.' She brought his head down to hers and kissed him with warmth he responded to in kind. 'You weren't in when I rang back last night,' she said gruffly when he raised his head.

'I had dinner with the Mayhews. By the time I picked up your message it was late and it seemed a shame to wake you. Were you out with Dido when I rang?'

'No, with Paddy Moran. He's the Ibsen fan you saw me with one night. We met for a coffee. Paddy's a financial adviser. I rang him to ask for his advice on the best way to invest the money for End House, and he suggested we meet near his bank for a chat before he caught his train home.'

James smiled wryly. 'It didn't occur to you to ask *my* advice?'

'Of course it did. But you've done so much for me already over End House I was determined not to impose on you again.'

'In future impose on me as much as you like.' James took her in his arms and kissed her at length, then raised his head to smile down into her flushed face. 'Last night

Nick Mayhew gave me the key to his house in the Cotswolds. Do you fancy a break from the city?'

As long as James took her with him Harriet didn't care where they went. 'I'd like that very much,' she said sedately. 'Thank you for my present,' she added and reached up to kiss him again.

'You've thanked me once already,' he said huskily, when he finally released her. 'Not that I'm counting.'

'Such a beautiful plant is surely worth more than one kiss,' she said demurely.

'In that case I'll bring orchids next time!'

She shook her head. 'I don't like orchids.'

'What a difficult woman you are. No orchids, no caviare, no champagne.'

'You should be grateful I'm so economical!'

Instead of the sleek, elegant car that she'd first seen outside End House, James drove Harriet to the Cotswolds in a chunky four-wheel drive.

'What happened to the Italian job you drove to Upcote?'

'This chap is better for the terrain we're heading for. Once we get out of this traffic,' added James as they crawled their way from one set of traffic lights to the next. 'We should have waited until Friday rush hour was over.'

'I don't mind,' said Harriet, and meant it. Feeling secure in her high perch in the solid vehicle, she couldn't have cared less about the noise and traffic and heat, simply because she was with James. Maybe this was what being in love was really about. Not just the sex and the excitement, but just being together. But by the end of the trip along the motorway and the more tortuous journey along country roads after it she was glad when James told her there was only a short distance to go. He took a minor road after Burford to a small village a couple of miles farther on until he reached a lane just past a church. He cruised down it slowly until he found a pair of open gates, and turned into a tree-lined drive that led to a house that looked more like a scaled down Edenhurst than the country cottage Harriet had expected.

'I was expecting something smaller,' she said when he swung her down.

'It was a rectory two centuries ago, connected by a path from the back garden to the church we passed back there. Nick bought the house quite recently, so it's still in process of renovation, with not much furniture to speak of.' James smiled at her as he unlocked a beautiful wooden door set in a stone arch. 'But apparently we have curtains, a kitchen, and somewhere to sit and sleep.'

'Perfect! Can I explore?'

'You can do anything you like. Lydia's instructions were to make ourselves at home. They've just spent the odd weekend here with the girls so far, but Nick intends retiring down here one day.'

All the rooms had the same panelling as the square hall, but the only one in use was a large sitting room with triple-light latticed windows looking out on a garden in urgent need of attention.

'Nick isn't much of a gardener,' said James, eyeing his surroundings with a look of nostalgia.

'Do you wish you'd been able to keep Edenhurst on as a home?' she asked with sympathy.

'Of course I do. But it's so much bigger than this it was never an option.' He shrugged philosophically. 'Have a look at the rest of it while I unpack the car.'

The large kitchen and the solitary upstairs bathroom had been modernised, but only two bedrooms were furnished. Harriet looked round with a smile as James joined her in the smaller room.

'This is obviously where your friend's daughters sleep.'

'Do *you* want to sleep here?' he said bluntly.

'No,' she said, equally direct. 'I took it for granted I'd share with you. Isn't that why we came?'

He touched a hand to her cheek. 'I'd be lying if I said it wasn't part of it. But there were other reasons. You looked so tired after your interior decorating I thought you needed a rest.' He smiled wryly. 'You don't like my London flat very much. And for obvious reasons I didn't think you'd fancy a weekend in the one at Edenhurst. I could have taken you to a hotel somewhere, but when Lydia suggested this place last night I was pretty sure you'd prefer it.'

'I do. It's lovely. Have you brought anyone else here?' she added casually.

'No. I've never been here before. Why?'

'Just curious.'

'Let's eat,' said James firmly, and led her down to the kitchen, where a large hamper kept company with a cool box on the table.

Harriet helped him unpack the food, her eyes widening as they stored away enough for the weekend with some left over.

'I put the wine to chill first of all,' he informed her.

'I hope it's not Barolo,' she said, laying the table.

James looked appalled. 'Certainly not. Only a barbarian would chill Barolo. Why don't you like it?'

Harriet pulled a face. 'Our delightful dinner party at La Fattoria put me off it for life.'

'For me it was the only thing bearable about the entire meal. You were so hostile towards me the food stuck in my throat. Your parting shot was the last straw,' James added as he carved a succulent joint of ham. 'Did you mean it?'

'I don't remember what I said,' she muttered, feeling her face grow hot.

'Oh, yes, you do,' he said, brandishing the carving knife

at her. 'You informed the company at large that it's unnecessary to like a man to want sex with him. Were you speaking from past experience, or just alluding to me?'

'I was hitting out at you.' Her chin lifted. 'Between you and Tim I felt cut to pieces that night, James Devereux.'

'You cut me back,' he said, and waved a dramatic hand at his chest. 'Right to the heart.'

'Then I'd better kiss it better,' said Harriet, her eyes gleaming as she strolled towards him. Greasy from the ham, he flung his hands wide as she slid one arm round his waist and began undoing his belt buckle and shirt buttons with the other.

'Harriet, that's not fair,' he said, breathing raggedly.

'All's fair in love and war,' she informed him, and kissed the taut, warm skin over his thudding heart.

'Which—is—this?' he said with difficulty.

'Both?' Harriet warmed to her task, teasing his bare back with her fingernails while her open mouth and flicking tongue moved up his chest to caress his flat nipples, then changed direction and moved slowly downwards until they reached the top button of his Levi's. She heard the sharp hiss of his breath as he sucked in his stomach muscles, and released him to stand back, her smile triumphant. 'You can wash your hands now.'

James let out the breath he'd been holding, his eyes blazing into hers for a moment before he turned away to lean, head bowed, over the sink, breathing hard as he ran hot water and detergent over his hands, then held his wrists under the cold tap. When he turned round he gave Harriet a smile that sent shivers down her spine. 'I'm hungry, otherwise I'd retaliate right now,' he informed her, buttoning his shirt. 'Instead I shall defer it to another time.'

'If you didn't like it I won't do it again!'

'You know damn well I liked it,' he growled. 'But I'd

like it a lot better with my hands free.' His eyes gleamed. 'So would you.'

They stared at each other for a long, sexually charged moment, then James smiled and she smiled back, and suddenly they were laughing, and bumping into each other in their rush to get the meal together.

For the first time since starting to paint her room Harriet felt hungry. Suddenly she was ravenous, and James nodded in approval as he cut thick slices of bread.

'That's better. It's time you started eating properly.'

'It was the paint. I didn't know I'd hate the smell of it so much. My grandmother had any decorating done while I was away in school.' She smiled at him happily, and then stopped dead, halfway through slicing a tomato.

'What is it?' he demanded.

Harriet looked at him in wonder for a moment. 'I just realised that for the first time since my grandmother died I feel utterly and completely happy.'

He sat very still. 'Why?' he said at last.

'Because I'm here with you,' she said simply.

James got up and walked round the table to pull her up into his arms and kiss her with tenderness she responded to with delight. 'I'm happy, too,' he said, raising his head, 'for the same reason.' He trailed a finger down her glowing cheek. 'Now finish your dinner like a good girl.'

'I'm always a good girl,' she said, sitting down, and then grinned at him. 'Well, mostly.'

To Harriet's surprise James gave her a parcel to open after dinner, when they were settled on the sofa in the sitting room.

'What is it?' she said, tearing paper aside to find half a dozen brand new novels from the best seller lists. 'Oh, James, how wonderful!'

'Have you read any of them?'

'Only the reviews,' she said, inspecting the titles. 'I wait until they come out in paperback.' She leaned up to kiss him, her eyes sparkling. 'You obviously don't intend boredom to be a problem this weekend.'

'You've got it all wrong. The books are to take home with you. While you're here with me I demand all your attention,' he informed her, and pulled her onto his lap. 'All of it. Starting now,' he whispered.

In Italy their lovemaking had been a tidal wave that swept over them without warning. Here, in this half-empty lamp-lit room, with the curtains drawn to enclose them in their own special world, the magic was different, but no less potent than in the moonlit tower where they'd first made love. This time James was in no rush, and Harriet melted against him with a murmur of pleasure as he kissed and caressed her with restraint all the more exciting because she knew that fire was held in check behind it. Fire, she knew, that would flare up and engulf them both in time, but for the moment just burned steadily, with a glow that permeated her entire body. Suddenly it flamed higher as his tongue found hers in a substitute penetration that triggered off immediate desire for the physical union they both yearned for with equal intensity.

James set Harriet on her feet and stood up, held her close for a moment, then took her hand and led her in silence up the dimly lit stairs to the dark bedroom. He reached out for a light switch but she stayed his hand, afraid that the sudden glare of the overhead light would destroy the magic.

He picked her up and walked in darkness to the bed, where he set her down with care, and leaned over her.

'There's a wall light here,' he whispered. 'I want to see you as we make love.'

Harriet kissed him by way of consent, and smiled at him when the intimate light of a rose-shaded lamp revealed the taut, beautiful male face above her, his eyes alight with an emotion she wanted so much to believe was love, not just the basic desire of a man desperate to mate.

James kissed her as he began to undress her, and she kissed him back as she helped him, and suddenly they were clumsy, panting and laughing as they fought with buttons and zips until at last their naked bodies were in contact, and the laughter died away. They held each other close until just holding was no longer enough, and James began tantalising her with swift, sweet, drinking kisses that moved from her mouth in a grazing, slow descent that filled Harriet with such unbearable expectation that at last she could bear no more.

'Please,' she gasped, but he held her still and continued on his downward path until his tongue penetrated her innermost hot recesses to find the hidden bud that sprang erect in response to his caress. Harriet moaned and tried to push him away, writhing in anguish because she didn't want this to happen yet, but it was coming and coming and she was helpless against the hot, delicious throbbing as he brought her to the climax she experienced alone.

Face flaming, Harriet scrambled away and turned her back on him, but James slid his arms round her and pulled her against him. He kissed the back of her neck, his hands cupping her breasts and caressing her nipples, rolling them between his fingertips, and she gave a smothered moan, and felt his erection nudge her and to her amazement found she was ready for him again. James flipped her over onto her back, slid his hands beneath her bottom and raised her, holding her there for a moment, then sheathed himself to the hilt, the look of fierce possession in his eyes heightening her pleasure as he withdrew slowly and thrust home again, and repeated the skilled manoeuvre again and again, each time a little faster and deeper, the frenzied rhythm culminating at last in release so overwhelming Harriet wondered if she'd died of it, until James kissed her to confirm she was alive before pulling up the covers to hold her in close embrace as she fell asleep.

For weather it was the worst weekend of the summer. For Harriet it was the best weekend of her life. The rain came down in torrents, and for two whole nights and days she never left the house except for a quick dash round the garden under an umbrella with James as a gesture to getting some fresh air. James went out both mornings for the daily paper to read together over the breakfast Harriet made while he was out. They did the crossword, drank coffee, then went back to bed to make love again and sleep until the need for food woke them up. And after a disgracefully late lunch the first day Harriet decided it was time to get a few things straight between them.

'James, about this relationship of ours—'

'Hallelujah!' he said in triumph. 'You actually admit that we have a relationship.'

'Of course I do.' She eyed him warily. 'But I'm not clear about the exact nature of it. You said you wanted me in your life—'

'Surely I've made that plain enough!' He paused, frowning. 'I assumed you wanted me in yours.'

'You assumed right,' she said impatiently. 'I thought I'd made that plain enough, too.'

James leaned across and took her hand. 'So what's the problem, darling?'

'You have a life of your own and so do I. Quite apart from Tim and Dido, I have friends I'm very fond of.' She looked at him in appeal. 'Even if you and I spend time together on a regular basis I still want—need—to go on seeing them.'

'Why on earth shouldn't you?' he said, surprised. 'My work takes me away from London quite a bit, so I don't expect you to sit at home at night, languishing until my return. As long as I get the lion's share of your time when I'm in town, of course,' he added.

'That goes without saying.' Harriet smiled at him luminously. 'Good. I'm glad that's settled. After all, I may need my friends one day.'

'And what day is that?' he demanded.

'When you and I are no longer in this relationship of ours.'

His eyes narrowed. 'You're so sure it won't last?'

Harriet smiled sadly. 'In my experience people I care for disappear from my life all too often.'

James frowned. 'I may be older than you, Harriet, but I'm not going to die just yet, I promise.'

'No. But you might tire of me.' She looked at him squarely. 'These things happen.'

'That's so unlikely it isn't worth discussing,' he said scornfully. 'But let's get something straight. You're happy to have me in your life, but you don't want to live with me. Am I right?'

'Try to see it from my viewpoint.' Harriet braced herself. 'I need time to get used to the idea of sharing my life with someone like you.'

'Someone like me,' James repeated. 'What do you mean by that?'

She sighed. 'I've had boyfriends in the past, until my double act with Tim ruled that out for a while, but I've never had a lover.'

He smiled as his hand tightened on hers. 'You've got one now.'

'I know.' She breathed in deeply. 'But it's hard to come to terms with that. I've never felt like this about anyone before.'

James got up, drawing her up with him. 'Maybe we should continue this on the sofa.' He put his arm round her as they crossed the hall to the sitting room, and kept it there as he drew her down to sit on his lap. 'Now tell me exactly how you feel.'

Harriet curled up against him as she tried to find the necessary words. 'I don't think I can be in love with you,' she said honestly.

His eyes narrowed. 'Why not?'

'Because Dido's been in love quite a lot—'

'With men other than my irresistible brother?'

Harriet nodded ruefully. 'She's always searching for someone like him.'

'She won't succeed,' James assured her. 'Hopefully there's only one Timothy Devereux.'

'Amen to that. Anyway, while she's in love with the current Mr Wrong she's so starry-eyed, she's blind to faults which seem all too apparent to me.' Harriet smiled apologetically. 'I don't feel like that about you.'

'You mean my faults are glaringly obvious?'

'I have good reason to know that you're kind and generous, but you're also impatient and autocratic sometimes. I can see all that clearly, but it doesn't alter the way I feel.'

'For God's sake, Harriet,' he said with sudden impatience. 'How do you feel?'

'Happy when I'm with you, and as though half of me is missing when you're not…' The rest of her words were smothered by a kiss that went on so long both of them were gasping for air when he let her go.

'I've known you since you were thirteen years old,' he said huskily, his hands in her hair to keep her looking up at him. 'I always disapproved of your relationship with Tim, but it was only when we met in Upcote that I realised why.' He smiled slowly, looking deep into her eyes. 'I wanted you myself.'

Harriet knew perfectly well that James Devereux wanted her. His way of showing it thrilled and delighted her. But she needed more than that before committing herself to a long-term relationship. Or even a short one. 'Are you in love with me, James?' she asked bluntly.

He looked at her in silence for a while, as though memorising her every feature. 'Yes,' he said at last. 'Utterly and completely and for as long as we both shall live.'

CHAPTER NINE

HARRIET gradually began to believe James meant every word, even during his absences, which were more often than either of them wanted. He went away regularly on his usual spot-check inspections at his properties, but spent the majority of his time at a new project his company was developing, which meant that sometimes a week, and even a fortnight, passed when Harriet didn't see him at all. But the time apart only made their reunions all the more passionate, their pleasure marred solely by the one main bone of contention between them.

When Harriet remained obdurate about moving in with him James finally came up with a suggestion. If his minimalist modern flat was the stumbling block he would buy her a house.

'I'll keep this flat as a showpiece,' he said as they sat together on one of his crescent-shaped sofas. 'In the meantime we'll look for something more to your taste.'

'It's not only the flat.' Harriet eyed him in appeal. 'I just feel it's too soon for us to live together anywhere quite yet.'

'Too *soon*!' James eyed her in exasperation. 'We've known each other for years, ten of them if you're counting.'

'But it's only recently that you've thought of me as anything but Tim's little chum,' Harriet reminded him.

'Tim's bride-to-be,' he corrected. 'Talking of brides, let's get this out in the open, Harriet. I have an idea that the real stumbling block for you is my take on marriage. Try to understand, darling. After my experience with Madeleine I'm superstitious about it. For me, and for her, too, it was the cure for love.' He cupped her face in his hands. 'I will love and cherish you for the rest of my natural life, I swear. Repeating that in a church won't make any difference.'

'You think I'm holding out for a wedding ring?' demanded Harriet, glaring at him.

'I seem to remember you stating certain views on the subject.'

'I was talking about commitment, not marriage.'

James sighed impatiently. 'And just what do you think I'm talking about? I'm offering you a home, financial security, and my humble self on a permanent basis. What else do you want?'

'Time.' Harriet gazed at him in appeal. 'This is too new. I'm still not used to the fact that you, well, that you—'

'I think love is the word you're looking for,' he said silkily. 'Pay attention. I love you, Harriet Verney.'

'I love you, too, James Devereux. But I'd rather leave any talk about a house until I'm sure.'

'Sure of your own feelings or mine?' he demanded.

'Neither. I just need to be sure it—this—won't end in tears.'

James smiled wryly. 'I probably will make you cry some time. Who knows, you may make me cry, too. But I'll also try my utmost to make you happy, darling.'

'You don't have to try. You just have to be with me to do that,' she assured him. 'Let's go on the way we are for a while,' she pleaded, when he'd stopped kissing her enough for her to speak. 'I couldn't care less about a wedding ring. But I like your version of courtship so much I just want to enjoy it a little longer before we actually live together.'

'When you smile at me like that I suppose you think I'll do anything you want,' he said, resigned, and pulled her on his lap. 'How long are you going to keep me waiting?'

Harriet snorted. 'I don't keep you waiting at all. You rushed me to bed tonight as soon as I got here.'

James gave her cheek an admonishing tap. 'I'm not talking about *making* love, great and glorious though it was just now. I have this desire, by no means unusual, to come home to you at night.'

'Don't expect me to have your slippers warming!'

He grinned. 'I don't wear slippers. To make me happy you just have to be here for me.'

'I work late sometimes.'

'Then I'll be here, waiting impatiently, for you.' James tipped her face up to his, his eyes gleaming triumphantly. 'Besides, when you give up that so-called studio flat of yours just think of the money you'll save on rent.'

'Oh, well!' Harriet laughed, and held up her hands in surrender. 'Why didn't you say that before? Let's start house-hunting tomorrow!'

The house-hunting had to be deferred for a while until James returned from troubleshooting at one of his hotels in Scotland. While he was away Harriet invited herself to supper in Bayswater to tell Dido her news, happy to kill two birds with one stone when Dido begged her to bring Tim along.

Dido was so delighted to see Tim she even managed to congratulate him on his forthcoming wedding. 'You've broken my heart, you monster,' she teased, and gave him a sisterly peck, then turned to hug Harriet. 'It's so lovely, with the three of us together again.'

Dido was right, thought Harriet as she kissed her friend. It was good to be back, now she didn't have to live here any more. Even with Tim talking non-stop about Francesca and his forthcoming nuptials over the meal.

'I expect you both to be there to hold my trembling hand,' he informed them.

'Try keeping me away!' said Dido happily, piling more food on his plate.

When the meal was over Harriet got to her feet, wine-glass in hand. 'Listen up, folks, now Tim's drawn breath for a moment I have an important announcement of my own to make...' She stopped dead, eyes wide in sudden panic and, to the utter horror of the other two, collapsed at their feet.

Harriet came round to the sound of Dido in tears, imploring her to wake up, and opened her eyes on Tim's desperately anxious face as he patted her cheek to bring her round.

'That's my girl,' he said soothingly. 'Up you come.' He helped her to her feet and settled her on the sofa, Dido fussing round them like a mother hen.

'Have some water, or wine, or something, Harriet,' she begged. 'I haven't got any brandy. Lord, you frightened us. What happened? You hardly drank anything.'

Harriet took in an unsteady breath. 'The room started spinning—then I suppose I passed out.'

Tim breathed in deeply, holding her hand. 'How do you feel?'

'Not very wonderful at the moment.' She smiled reassuringly at Dido. 'I'd love some tea.'

Dido leapt into action. 'Right away, love.'

When she was out of earshot in the kitchen Tim gave Harriet a searching look. 'Are you cooking up for some virus? You look hellish peaky.'

'I feel peaky.' She shivered. 'I've never fainted before.'

'I'd be grateful if you never do it again in my company, either! When's Jed coming back?'

'Tomorrow or Saturday, he's not sure yet.'

'Make sure you take it easy this weekend.' He grinned. 'I'm sure Jed won't mind if you want to spend most of it in bed.'

'Bed is exactly where I want to be right this minute,' she said shakily, wishing a magic wand could waft her to her own, there and then.

'Dido will want you to spend the night here,' he warned.

He was right. Dido was loud with protests when Harriet insisted on going back to Clerkenwell.

'I'm fine now,' she assured her anxious friend.

'Don't worry, Dido,' said Tim, utterly serious for once. 'I shall make sure the invalid is safely tucked up in bed with her phone before I go off to my place.'

He was as good as his word. When they got back to the flat he made tea while Harriet undressed in her bathroom, and then saw her into bed.

'Just before you passed out,' he reminded her, 'you were about to make an announcement, one of some import, I fancy.'

Harriet's eyes lit up. 'So I was. James and I are going to live together, Tim. I don't like his flat so he's going to buy a house, and I get to choose it.'

Tim hugged her in delight. 'You're going to be my sister-in-law!'

She detached herself gently. 'No, Tim. I'm moving in with James, not marrying him.'

His expressive face fell. 'Why the hell not?'

'Madeleine,' she said tersely.

'She's history. Why should you be worried about *her*?'

'I'm not. James is. After marriage with Madeleine he's sure it's the cure for love.'

Tim frowned. 'Do you agree with that?'

'No. But I can see his point.'

'How about you, pet? Would you *like* to marry Jed?'

'No,' said Harriet, so positively Tim looked taken aback.

'Oh, right, as long as you both feel the same.' He bent to kiss her goodnight. On his way to the door he turned, wagging a finger. 'If you feel strange again, ring me, and I'll drop everything and rush to the rescue, *ventre á terre.*'

She laughed. 'Nice thought, but you need a horse to race belly to the ground.'

Tim didn't smile back. 'Seriously, I meant what I said. Take care, Harry. Please.'

Harriet felt tearful when he'd gone, overcome by a sudden longing for her grandmother's practical, comforting presence. But because Olivia Verney had disapproved of tears Harriet blew her nose, dried her eyes and settled down early to the sleep she seemed to need so much of lately.

Next morning she slept later than usual, and woke feeling perfectly normal. She rushed off to work without breakfast, but coped with her usual busy day at the agency with a zest remarked on by her colleagues. Teased about the new man in her life, Harriet gleefully hugged her secret to herself. Her man wasn't new at all. But at thirteen she'd had no idea that one day James Devereux would be the most important thing in her life. Euphoric at the thought of seeing him later, she worked flat out all day so she could leave in time to go shopping for a celebration dinner, then hurried home to the message she knew would be waiting for her.

'I'll be with you sometime this evening, as soon as the traffic allows,' James informed her. 'I've missed you, darling. Have you missed me?'

Oh, yes. Her eyes gleamed as she thought of ways to show him later exactly how much she had missed him.

The disadvantage of living in one room meant constant vigilance to keep it tidy, and she'd left in such a rush first thing there was work to be done before James arrived. Harriet whirled like a dervish through some household chores before her shower. While her hair dried she scrubbed potatoes and sliced green beans, mixed a spoonful of horse-radish into clotted cream and left it to chill alongside the poached salmon waiting in the fridge. She finished off her hair with a hot brush, made up her face and sprayed herself with perfume, and after a moment's indecision pulled on white cotton drawstring trousers and the caramel vest top she'd worn the first time James had kissed her.

Harriet was searching for shoes when James knocked on her door.

'Someone was leaving the building as I arrived,' he called. 'Let me in.'

Harriet threw open the door, smiling at him in such radiant welcome James dumped down his briefcase, kicked the door shut and swept her off her bare feet to whirl her round a couple of times, then kissed her until her head reeled. When he put her down at last Harriet gave a despairing little moan and crumpled into the arms that shot out to catch her.

When she came round she was lying on the sofa looking up into James' shocked, haggard face.

'Darling,' he said hoarsely, and touched a shaking hand to her cheek. 'What happened?'

'I've been rushing, and then you spun me around,' she said faintly. 'Hold me tight, please.'

James carefully lifted her onto his lap and held her close. 'Have you been going without food while I'm away?' he accused.

'No. And before you ask I've been to bed early every night except Tuesday when Dido asked me to supper. Tim came, too.'

'Brave man. Did he manage to escape unscathed from her clutches?' he asked, relaxing a little.

Harriet smiled. 'Dido's finally come to terms with the fact that he's well and truly spoken for.' But she made no mention of the previous faint. James looked worried enough as it was. There was no point in worrying him even more.

'Are you feeling better now?' he asked, kissing her hair.

'Much better. I must see to dinner.'

'To hell with dinner. We'll pick something up on the way home.'

'No,' said Harriet, and despite his violent protests got to her feet, and stayed on them without mishap. 'I just have to cook a few vegetables.'

'Then I'll just have to stand over you while you do,' said James inexorably.

He was as good as his word, and hovered over her until in the end Harriet told him to go and sit down before she did him an injury.

'This is no place for two people to work together.'

'Or even for one person to live in,' he said, surveying the room with a pejorative eye. 'We spend the rest of the weekend at the flat, and no arguments, please.'

'OK,' said Harriet, with a docility that won her a look of deep suspicion. 'What?' she demanded.

'You must be feeling worse than I thought.'

'I'm fine. And I'm perfectly happy to spend the weekend at your place.' She gave him a look that brought him to his feet again. 'I've missed you so much, James, I don't care where we are as long as we're both in the same place.'

He started towards her, then stopped and stepped back, his eyes glittering. 'If I show my thanks in the time-honoured way, darling, the dinner might spoil. And after the episode just now some food is a good idea for you. Me, too,' he added, and smiled. 'To quote Tim, I'm hungry.'

James rang for a cab after the meal, and told Harriet to get her things together. 'I'll do the washing up,' he informed her, grumbling at the lack of a dishwasher. 'And there's no point in buying one because you won't be living here much longer.'

'Not so fast! If I give the flat up at this stage I won't get my deposit back.'

James shrugged impatiently. 'What does that matter? I'll cover any loss.'

'No.' She shook her head as she zipped up her bag.

'Why not?'

'I won't accept money from you.'

He took the bag from her and picked up his briefcase as the bell rang. 'When we live together, Harriet, you won't have much option.'

'Maybe not. But that's in the future.'

'Not too far in the future,' he assured her. 'Give me one good reason why we should waste time apart?'

When they arrived at his apartment Harriet waited until James switched on the lights, then went straight to the far wall and pressed the button that slid the panel back to reveal the spare room.

'Are you making some kind of statement?' demanded James, close behind her.

'No, I had this bright idea while you were away,' she said absently, studying the room. 'I have a suggestion to make.'

'You want to sleep here tonight?'

Harriet turned to surprise open dismay in his eyes. 'No, of course not,' she said impatiently. 'I want to sleep with you.' She smiled with deliberate invitation. 'After you've made love to me half the night, of course.'

James caught her in his arms. 'I might if you're good! So tell me about this request.'

'If we don't find somewhere else to live for a while, could I use this room when I move in here? If I had a sofa and a small television I could use it as a sort of snug when you're away. Your living room is just too big and minimalist for me to feel comfy.'

'If you're willing to move out of that dump you call a flat and in here you can have anything you want,' he assured her.

'Only until we find a house,' she reminded him, and laughed suddenly.

'What now?'

'In one breath I was refusing your money, and in the next happily splurging it on extra furniture and a new house. Am I illogical or what?'

'I like illogical women. Come to bed.'

'Your seduction technique could use some work,' she informed him as he hustled her through the big, uncluttered room. 'I thought we might watch television for a bit,' she complained as they passed the huge plasma screen.

'We can do that later—much later,' said James, and as if his patience had suddenly run out he picked her up, strode into the other room and deposited her in the middle of his bed.

Harriet lay watching him as he shrugged out of his jacket and tore off his tie. 'I love you, James,' she said quietly, and he stopped dead halfway through unbuttoning his shirt.

'I love you, too, my darling.' He discarded the shirt and knelt on the bed to draw her up against him. 'You frightened the hell out of me tonight. Don't do that again, please.'

'I'll try,' she said against his bare chest, and listened to his heart thudding against hers as he held her closer.

With an effort he put her away from him. 'You know I want to make love to you, but—'

'No buts. I want it, too,' she said fiercely.

'Are you up to it after fainting like that?'

'Yes. Are you?' she whispered and stroked a caressing hand down over his chest and lower still, to the place where lightweight grey fabric covered the exact extent of his readiness. 'If you're not,' she added, 'maybe I can persuade you.' She slid from the bed, undid the drawstring and stepped out of the trousers, then stripped off the vest top and dropped it on the floor. She saw James swallow hard, and smiled as she slowly revolved in front of him. 'The underwear was a present. Do you like it?'

James drew in a deep, shuddering breath, and showed his appreciation by tossing her on the bed and removing the present with ungentle hands. 'Who gave it to you?' he growled as the rest of his clothes hit the floor.

'One of my gentlemen friends,' she said rashly, then gasped as he dived on her and swept her hands wide.

'Which one?' he demanded, his eyes blazing into hers.

'Tim, of course.'

'Why the hell should my brother give you underwear?' he said, incensed.

'It was a *present*. Francesca picked it out for him in Paris.' Harriet swallowed. 'James, kiss me.'

He released her hands at once and his eyes glittered. 'Where?'

'All over,' she sighed, and stretched in invitation against him.

They slept late next morning, and lingered over breakfast before they went shopping for furniture.

'I rang Whitefriars Estates while you were in the bath,' said James. 'I told them we need a reasonable garden and plenty of space and so on. They'll send me some brochures.'

Harriet gave him a warning look as they got in the car. 'I want something more on the lines of End House than Edenhurst, James Devereux.'

'*We*,' he corrected her, 'need a home. And soon. In the meantime let's look at furniture.'

If Harriet had harboured any doubts about sharing her life with James Devereux so soon, they were gone for good by the end of the day. Up to that point their time together had been purely social, but shopping with him, for furniture and a television first, and food later, delighted her by being such fun. They got back to the flat at last, laden with bags, still laughing about the elegant young man who'd given them an unnecessarily hard sell about the sofa Harriet set her heart on the moment she set eyes on it.

'*Exquisitely* comfortable, adjustable to several angles, and in such *butter*-soft leather,' said Harriet, giggling. 'This shade is perfect for madam's hair. Black is *so* last year.'

James laughed and kissed her hair in passing as he stored food away. 'I admit that your choice surprised me.'

'It gave you heart failure, you mean, at that price, especially when you insisted on the chair and that cute footstool thing to go with it.'

'A small price to pay to tempt you into my lair.' He smiled a little. 'But I did expect you to go for something more traditional.'

'And clash with all this stark elegance? Certainly not.'

James took her by the shoulders. 'If you want flowery chintz, or feel a desperate urge for girly cushions, I don't care a damn as long as you come here to live with me. And be my love,' he added softly.

Harriet looked up at him in silence for a moment, her eyelashes damp. 'This is so hard to believe sometimes, James. You and me, I mean.'

'It is for me now and then,' he admitted, 'but only when we're apart. When we're together it feels so right I wonder how I existed without you all these years.'

Harriet buried her face against his shoulder, soaking his shirt with tears she couldn't keep back. 'Sorry,' she said thickly. 'Lord knows why I'm crying.'

'Then stop it at once,' he said huskily. 'I can't handle it.'

She sniffed inelegantly. 'Give me some tissues, please, and then I'll make tea.'

James mopped her up, and ordered her to sit down on one of the crescent sofas. 'You look tired. Switch on the television we never got round to watching last night and *I'll* make tea.'

The weekend was all the more wonderful to Harriet because James hadn't made it back from Scotland for the previous one. And, just as Tim had predicted, his brother was not at all averse to spending a great deal of this weekend in bed.

'Not just to make love to you,' he informed Harriet as he set up the new television in his bedroom. 'We both need the rest.'

'I thought that television was for my snug,' she reminded him as she watched the operation.

James scrolled through the various channels until he was satisfied, then smiled at her smugly. 'I'll borrow it until you move in. Or maybe even buy another one for the spare room,' he added as two English batsmen came out for the last session of the day.

'Ah, cricket!' Harriet laughed. 'No wonder you were so keen to lug it back here yourself today!'

'They couldn't deliver before Monday, and the test match may be over by then,' James said absently, his eyes on the wicket.

'You could have watched it on the mega screen out there,' she pointed out.

He grinned. 'I'll enjoy it a lot more in bed with you.'

'A good thing I like cricket, then.'

'I was the one who taught you how to hold a bat, remember.' James took her in his arms. 'Cricket is only one of the many things you and I have in common, my darling. We were made for each other.'

Because James was going away for the week to check on the transformation of a Gothic mansion into a super luxury hotel, Harriet stayed over for the first time on the Sunday night and let James drop her off at work next morning on his way to pick up Nick Mayhew for the drive to the north of England.

Giles Kemble eyed her holdall with interest. 'Good weekend, Harriet?'

She smiled at him radiantly. 'Perfect!'

The week that followed was anything but. As it wore on it became an endurance test for Harriet. The phone calls from James each night were the only high spots of days that seemed endless as she struggled with fatigue, which increased as she worked late most evenings to keep on top of her workload. Tim came round one evening to announce that he was off to see Francesca over the weekend, but he left early when Harriet couldn't control her yawns.

'You look as though you could do with a good night's sleep, my girl. Surely you got *some* over the weekend?'

'Of course I did,' she said, flushing.

'When are you actually moving in with Jed?'

'Soon.' She told him about the new furniture for the spare room.

'Good God! He *must* be crazy about you,' said Tim, impressed. 'He thinks the place is perfect the way it is.' He frowned. 'And where am I supposed to sleep when I stay over, may I ask?'

'Where you always sleep. Your bed's still there.' She smiled. 'I sleep with James, remember.'

'I still can't get my head round that.' He gave her a hug. 'Goodnight, angel.'

During his nightly phone call James told Harriet to go straight to his apartment the following evening and wait for him. 'Don't worry about dinner. We'll order in.'

The wait for James that Friday night seemed endless. Harriet stood at one of the big arched windows, gazing down blindly at the river, feeling hot and cold by turns. Excitement and delight gradually gave way to dread, which seeped icily along her nerves until she was on the point of bolting by the time James finally arrived. He strode in, his smile fading as, instead of hurling herself into his arms as usual, she stayed rooted to the spot.

He seized her by the shoulders to kiss her, and straightened slowly, frowning at her lack of response. 'Darling, what's the matter? You look shattered. Have you been fainting again?' he demanded.

'Just once,' said Harriet.

'Have you seen a doctor?' he said urgently.

'Yes, this afternoon.' She stepped back, her dark-ringed eyes fastened on his. 'I thought I had some virus, but apparently I'm having a baby.'

James stared at her in shocked silence that grew to unbearable proportions before he found his voice, and asked the question she'd been dreading.

'Is it mine, Harriet?'

CHAPTER TEN

A WAVE of such anguish engulfed her at his words Harriet felt physically sick. 'No, it's not.' She took fierce satisfaction in watching the blood drain from James Devereux's haggard face. 'It's mine.'

She took her phone from her bag and rang for a taxi, then tossed his door key on the counter, but before she could make it to the door he barred her way.

'Where the hell do you think you're going?' he demanded furiously. 'You can't throw something like that at me and just take off.'

She gave him a flaying look. 'Just watch me!'

'I'm entitled to an explanation, Harriet. Now,' he snapped.

'What is there to explain?'

'How this happened.'

'In the usual way, of course,' she said wearily.

James took a deep breath, fighting to get his emotions under control. 'You told me you took the pill.'

'I do.'

'Did you miss a day?'

'No. Nor did I take antibiotics, have a stomach upset, or do anything else to stop them working. But the single-hormone pill fails in one or two cases out of a hundred. I didn't realise I was one of the unlucky statistics.' Her mouth twisted. 'I was strongly advised to give you the glad news, but I wish to God I'd kept it to myself now.'

'Who advised you?' he demanded, looking so grim she wanted to run. 'Who else knows about this?'

'No one except the doctor I saw today. She said that a

148

father always has a right to know. True, of course. But you obviously doubt that you are the father, so get out of my way, please, I want to go home.'

'Home?' said James scathingly, ignoring the rest of her tirade. 'That one-room glory-hole in Clerkenwell?'

'After your gut reaction to the news, James,' she said bitterly, 'your opinion of where I live is irrelevant. Let me pass, please.'

'Like hell I will.' He took her by the shoulders, his eyes narrowing dangerously when she cringed from him. 'For God's sake stop that, Harriet. You've got to let me help you.'

'Whether you're the father or not?' she threw at him, then swallowed convulsively, her eyes widening in panic as her stomach heaved. Beads of perspiration broke out on her upper lip, and she threw James an agonised look as she fled to the kitchen sink. She gesticulated wildly for him to go away, but he kept an arm round her and put a cool, supporting hand on her forehead while she threw up.

Coughing and gasping in utter misery, Harriet scrubbed at her eyes and wiped her nose on kitchen paper, then sipped the glass of mineral water James gave her.

'Where are your things?' he asked, when he returned from paying off her taxi.

'I didn't bring any.'

'You can have something of mine. I'll fetch your clothes tomorrow,' he said, and picked her up.

Harriet struggled wildly, but he held her fast.

'I'm putting you to bed whether you like it or not,' he said roughly, his face grim with determination as he strode off with her.

'I'm going to be sick again!' she gasped, and James raced to his bathroom and held her head again while she retched until her ribs ached.

Wishing she could just die and get it over with, Harriet

straightened eventually, shuddering as she saw her ashen face in the mirror. She turned her back on it in disgust, and pushed James away as he bent to pick her up.

'Don't *do* that. It makes me dizzy.'

Apparently convinced she would collapse without some kind of support, James put an arm round her waist again and took her into the other room. He sat her down on the bed, and crossed the room to slide back the section of wall that hid his wardrobe. He took out T-shirt and boxers, and put them down beside her. 'Shall I help you undress?'

'No, thank you, I'll manage.' If it killed her, she added silently as he left the room, which was showing a disquieting tendency to revolve. Illusion due to the curved walls, she assured herself. But when she stood up the floor undulated beneath her feet like the deck of a ship, and she sat down again sharply.

James knocked on the door. 'Are you in bed yet?'

'No.'

'May I come in?' he called.

'It's your bedroom.'

James put his head round the door. 'What's wrong?'

Was he serious? 'I feel sick, giddy and utterly miserable—and I'm pregnant,' she added bitterly. 'Otherwise I'm just dandy.'

For once in his life James Devereux looked at a complete loss. 'What do you want me to do?'

Kiss me better, she thought despairingly. 'I'm afraid you'll have to help me undress, after all.'

James crossed to the bed and knelt to take off her shoes. 'Heels like these are a bad idea in the circumstances,' he said tightly.

'I didn't know about the ''circumstances'' until I saw the doctor. This afternoon,' she added, in case he'd missed the point.

James hadn't. His mouth twisted as he got up. 'It must have been a hell of a shock, Harriet.'

'It was. I thought I had some kind of flu.' She began to unbutton her black linen suit jacket. 'This bit I can do. It was the standing up part that beat me.'

James took the jacket from her and with infinite care, as if she were attached to a stick of gelignite, swung her feet up and laid her back against the stacked pillows. 'Undo your shirt.'

Harriet did so clumsily, all fingers and thumbs under the tense eyes watching every movement. 'Hold your arms up,' he instructed when she'd finished, and she obeyed, face burning as he tossed her once crisp pink shirt aside.

James shifted her enough to unfasten her bra and remove it so he could slip his T-shirt over her head. By the time he put her back against the pillows his hands were shaking and he looked as hot and bothered as Harriet.

'Now for the skirt,' he said, clearing his throat.

She unhooked it and slid the zip down and James drew the skirt away, his jaw suddenly clenched at the sight of lace-topped stockings. As he slowly peeled them off Harriet found her voice.

'Not the knickers,' she said gruffly.

'Right.' He drew the quilt up over her legs, his face rigidly blank. 'What else can I do for you?'

'Just go away, please,' she said wearily, and turned her face into the pillows.

Harriet woke later to find it was nearly two hours since she'd sprung her bombshell on James. She sat up with care, and crawled gingerly out of bed. Her head still felt like a balloon about to float away, but at least her legs seemed willing to hold her up. She lingered in the bathroom for a while in case there was any throwing up to be done, decided there wasn't, washed her pallid face, dragged a comb through her hair and went back into the bedroom.

James was waiting for her, still dressed in formal shirt and suit trousers. 'I heard you moving about,' he said stiffly. 'I thought you might need me.'

'No, I don't.' She gave him an icy look as she got back into bed. 'Now or in the future.'

His eyes glittered ominously. 'You're never going to forgive me?'

Harriet shrugged. 'You know that some of my friends are men, and as a wild card there's even Tim to bring into it if you're keeping score, so I suppose you can be forgiven for questioning rightful paternity. But not by me,' she added flatly.

'Harriet, will you just listen?' said James with sudden violence. 'You've got it wrong. It's not long since we became lovers, so when you said you were pregnant I was bloody terrified that the child *was*n't mine, not that it was!'

Harriet desperately wanted to believe him, but his initial doubt had cut so deep she couldn't. She raised a sardonic eyebrow. 'Or maybe were you "bloody terrified" that I'd played the oldest trick in the book to get you to marry me.'

'It never crossed my mind,' he retorted, so emphatically Harriet gave him a mocking smile.

'Methinks the gentleman doth protest too much.' She shrugged. 'Don't worry, James. I didn't come here to propose.'

His eyes hardened. 'That's usually a male prerogative.'

'You would know. Did you go on bended knee to Madeleine?'

'No. I'm not going on bended knee to you, either, Harriet.' He sat on the edge of the bed and took her hand. 'But I am asking you to marry me.'

'How kind.' Harriet detached her hand. 'Thank you, James. But the answer's no.'

'You haven't thought this through,' he said with sudden passion, a pulse throbbing beside his mouth. 'This isn't just about you, Harriet. There's a child involved. Our child—'

'You're sure about that?'

'Of course I'm sure,' he said scornfully. 'Otherwise why would you have told me?'

'I could be palming another man's child off on you.'

James eyed her with distaste. 'This isn't a joke, Harriet.'

'Dead right it's not,' she agreed. 'But I'm in the mood to lash out at someone.'

'And I'm the nearest.' To Harriet's surprise he smiled a little. 'But not dearest right now.'

She looked away. 'I'm not lashing out at you because of the baby—'

'Our baby,' he said very deliberately. 'Now lie still for a while. I'm going to have a quick shower and make some supper.' He got up to take some clothes from the wardrobe. 'While I'm doing that you can mull over the idea of lawful wedlock.'

Once she heard the water running Harriet sat up cautiously, wondering where he'd put her clothes. But when she put her feet to the floor it was obvious that making a run for it wasn't an option. She subsided against the pillows again, defeated. She would have to stay put and go home tomorrow. But that was the hell of it. James was right. The Clerkenwell flat wasn't home. Neither was the one in Bayswater, and in any case Dido's sister was moving in there shortly. The plus in her life was the money for End House, which was no fortune, but at least she wouldn't be penniless when she had to give up her job. The minus factor was a total lack of relatives and nowhere to call home.

James emerged from the bathroom in jeans and the twin to the T-shirt Harriet was wearing. 'How do you feel?'

'Depressed,' she said morosely.

'You need food.'

'No way,' she said in a panic. 'I need a bath, not food.'

'Right. I'll find you another shirt.'

James helped Harriet out of bed, waited until he was sure she could stand unaided then let her get to the bathroom in her own time while he turned on the shower to the correct temperature.

'Make do with a shower tonight,' he ordered. 'Do you need help?'

'No.'

'Leave the door ajar. Shout if you want me,' said James, and left her to it.

Harriet used James' shampoo on her hair, and lathered herself with his shower gel and then stood for a long time under the jet of water, one hand smoothing her stomach as she came to terms with the fact that there was a life in there.

'Time to come out, Harriet,' said James.

She switched off the water and took the towelling robe he held out, amused when he kept his face averted. 'It's all right, James. You've seen me naked before.'

'I know damn well I've seen you naked before.' His eyes burned into hers as he handed her a towel to rub her hair. 'This evening has been more of a strain for me than for you in some ways.'

'And just how do you work that out?' she demanded.

'You felt ill while I was undressing you. I, unfortunately, was in my usual rude health. Must I draw pictures?'

'Even though you'd just seen me throwing up?' she said astonished.

'Yes,' he said, the glint in his eyes bringing colour to her face. 'The stockings were the last straw. Now do you want to go back to bed?'

'I feel better in bed,' she admitted, 'but…' She trailed into silence and looked away.

'I can sleep in the spare room if that's your problem.'

'Thank you. I'd prefer that.'

'I was sure you would,' he said tersely, and made for the door. 'I didn't do anything about food earlier in case the smell penetrated in here and made you ill again. Could you cope now if I made myself an omelette?'

'Yes, as long as you don't make one for me.'

'Are you sure there's nothing you want, Harriet?'

She thought for a moment. 'After you've had supper would you make me some tea?'

'I'll make it now,' he said promptly.

'No. I'll enjoy it much more after I've brushed my teeth and dried my hair and so on. But at my current energy level this could take some time.'

'Have you eaten anything today?'

'Not since breakfast. My visit to the doctor early this afternoon put me right off lunch.'

His jaw clenched. 'And of course you worked for the rest of the afternoon?'

'With mind-numbing industry,' she agreed acidly.

Heat flared in the tawny eyes for an instant before James turned on his heel and made for the door. 'I won't be long. Shout if you want me.'

It was amazing what feeling clean could do, thought Harriet as she finally made it into the bed James had re-arranged for her. Unfortunately she was also pregnant, which meant some serious thinking now James had asked her to marry him. This was by no means unexpected. James Devereux had always shouldered his responsibilities. But there was no way she could accept a man who not only harboured doubts about this particular responsibility, but hated the thought of marrying again.

Harriet told James this when he brought her tea accompanied by some toast she found to her surprise that she quite fancied.

He placed the tray on the steel and glass table beside the

bed, handed her a plate of toast, then poured tea into a tall white mug as he heard her out.

'My turn now, Harriet,' he said, when she'd finished. He sat on the edge of the bed and looked at her with disquieting intensity. 'When I found you in the tower room that night my brain shut down at the sight of you in my bed. I forgot the protection I always carry with me, forgot that you belonged to Tim. I forgot everything other than the desperate desire to make love to you. So the responsibility is mine. Eat your toast,' he added.

Harriet nibbled warily, trying to hide how deeply his words affected her. 'Odd that the pills didn't work, either,' she said at last.

'Presumably they have done in the past?' asked James casually.

'They haven't been put to the test much. The one time I really fancied myself in love my hero objected to my closeness to Tim, and dumped me a few months into the relationship—if you could call it that. I was so humiliated I jumped at the chance to salvage my pride when Tim suggested the fake engagement.'

'And saved you for me in the process.' James smiled triumphantly. 'You didn't stand a chance, Harriet. Fate obviously meant you to marry me.'

'You hate the thought of marriage,' she reminded him.

'With you—and you alone—I can cope with matrimony.'

She shook her head. 'No, James.'

'Yes, Harriet. Living together isn't enough.' He took the mug from her and placed it with precision on the tray, then took her hand in a firm grasp. 'A child alters everything. Antiquated though it may be I want my child—and his mother—to have my name. So for the second time of asking will you marry me?'

She looked at him in sombre silence. 'If cohabiting isn't

enough for you I may have to swallow my pride and say yes. You know my situation only too well, James.'

He shrugged. 'There is another option. If you really can't face the thought of marrying me I can still buy you the house with a garden.'

Her eyes narrowed. 'And you would live here and I would live there, wherever "there" might be?'

'As I said, it's an option.' He released her hand. 'It's not what I want, but it's something for you to think about.'

Harriet thought about it so much she couldn't get to sleep. The night before she'd been so happy at the thought of seeing James again, and for a while she'd been even happier today at the thought of having his baby. Then the doubts had crept in as she waited to give him the news. And her doubts had been justified. His reaction had turned her life upside down. Not your fault, she whispered, patting her stomach. In the normal way of things she would have been euphoric about having James' baby. But not like this—forcing him to marry her. She didn't care for his other suggestion, either. The thought of living alone and pregnant in some house in the suburbs was even less appealing than in her studio flat.

At three in the morning Harriet gave up trying to sleep. She switched on the bedside lamp and got out of bed, opened the door quietly and peered out into the living room, which looked even bigger by night, with only the city lights outside to light her way. She stole barefoot across the cool, uncarpeted floor to the kitchen area, wondering if she could manage to butter some bread without putting lights on to disturb James. But before she reached her goal the door to the spare room slid back and he hurried towards her, shrugging on a dressing gown.

'Harriet, do you feel ill?' he demanded, and switched on the lights over the central island.

'No, I'm hungry, not ill—sorry I woke you up.'

His dark-ringed eyes captured hers. 'Do you imagine I was asleep?'

She looked away. 'For obvious reasons I couldn't sleep, either. Do you mind if I make myself something to eat?'

'For God's sake, Harriet,' he snapped, 'do you have to ask?'

'Yes,' she said simply. 'I do.'

James breathed in deeply, very obviously trying not to lose his temper. 'Go back to bed. What would you like? More toast?'

She inclined her head graciously. 'Lovely. That's very kind of you.'

'*Kind?*' he said through his teeth. 'Go.'

Harriet went. When she got back to James' room she remade the bed and settled back against the pillows, hoping he'd make her a lot of toast.

When James arrived, after a longer interval than promised, he had himself well in hand and the toast he brought was piled with glossy, perfectly scrambled eggs. 'No nonsense,' he said sternly. 'You need to eat.'

'Yes, James,' said Harriet meekly, and the moment he was through the door fell ravenously on the food, and only by superhuman effort managed to leave one square of egg-crowned toast uneaten by the time he came back.

'Eat it all, please,' he ordered as he set a mug of tea beside her.

She gave a martyred sigh and, with James standing over her, slowly finished the last piece as though she were conferring a favour. 'There,' she said, handing him the plate. 'Thank you. Perfect scrambled eggs,' she added with justice.

'When Tim was ten, and unhappy, sometimes it was all he'd eat, and sometimes I was the only one around to cook it, so it's my signature dish,' said James. 'These days Tim's tastes are more sophisticated.'

'He's gone to Florence this weekend,' said Harriet, sipping her tea.

'I know.' He shot her a look. 'It's not long to his wedding. Are you going to let me pay for your air fare?'

'No, thank you, James. I can manage that myself.'

'I don't know why I bothered to ask,' he said savagely. 'Is there anything else you need tonight?'

'Nothing at all.'

'In that case we'll leave further discussion until tomorrow. Hopefully, you'll feel better disposed by then to the sensible solution to our situation.'

She gave him a mocking smile. 'If you're alluding to marriage do try for a more attractive way to describe it, James. First it's the cure for love, now it's a sensible solution.'

His eyes took on a dangerous gleam. 'For you and me, and our child, it's the *only* solution, Harriet. By the way,' he added as he took clothes from his wardrobe. 'I'm going out early in the morning. We need food. I'll try not to wake you, but if I do, stay in bed until I get back. Now try to sleep. Goodnight.'

Harriet slept eventually, but woke early to listen for James. It seemed like hours before she heard him leave the spare room. She lay with eyes closed in case he looked in, and at long last heard the outer door close behind him. She slid carefully out of bed, relieved when the room held still and her legs held firm. She took her phone from her handbag and rang for a taxi, and soon afterwards, with only teeth brushed and hair combed by way of grooming, she was in a cab on her way to Clerkenwell. When she got to the flat she changed her clothes and collected the weekend bag she'd packed the day before, in that other lifetime before she'd seen a doctor. And only then left a message for James on his phone at the flat.

'I need some time to myself. I'm not in Clerkenwell or

with Dido, so don't try to look for me, and please don't worry. I feel much better today, and I'm perfectly safe. I'll ring you tomorrow.'

She knew perfectly well that James would worry. But right now she didn't care. She needed time to herself to put her life in order before she saw him again. It was cruel, maybe, but she just couldn't forget those three little words that had cut her to the heart. Nor did she believe for one minute the explanation he'd made for them. Harriet's eyes hardened. For a split second James had doubted that her child was his.

After several hours of such hard thinking her brain threatened to shut down, Harriet curled up on a sofa later that afternoon to watch an old Hollywood musical on television. In a break in the music she heard footsteps in the hall and shot to her feet, heart pounding, looking round wildly for something to use as a weapon.

But the man who strode into the untidy room was no burglar. James Devereux glared at her furiously, dangling a key in front of her eyes. 'I've got one of these, too. Tim's only just told me that the other two are on holiday, so I never thought of his house. I hope you're pleased with yourself, lady. I rang Dido before Tim, so you've sent three people off their heads with worry.'

'*You* worried the others. I rang you to say I was safe,' she said, and took her phone from her bag to reassure her friend, who was in such a state it took Harriet some time to calm her down. 'I'm fine, Dido, honestly,' she said at last. 'Come to my place for supper on Monday evening.'

James came in from the hall, snapping his own phone shut as she finished. 'I've just let Tim know he can enjoy the rest of his weekend in peace.'

'You can do the same, now,' said Harriet, and sat down on the sofa again, only to be hauled summarily to her feet.

'You're coming with me,' James informed her grimly. 'Now,' he added in a tone that dared her to disobey.

She might as well, she decided as she repacked her bag in Tim's chaotic bedroom. She'd done her thinking and made up her mind, which had been her main object in coming here. She would put James in the picture once they got back to the apartment.

When she went downstairs James took her bag from her, made sure the house was secure, and then drove her home in silence, his face set in such angry lines Harriet couldn't imagine telling him anything for a while. He helped her out in the basement car park and marched her over to the lift. When they got to his floor he unlocked his door, dumped her bag down and seized her wrist to lead her to the spare bedroom.

Harriet felt a sharp stab of compunction when she saw that the room had been rearranged to make space for the new chestnut leather sofa and chair. 'It arrived, then.'

'Delivered this morning, as I ordered,' James informed her. 'I went out early to make sure I was on hand when it came. I wasn't long, but you were too quick for me. I suppose you took off the moment I left.'

'Yes. I needed time to myself to think.'

'Is that the truth, Harriet?'

She frowned, taken aback by his air of desperation. 'Of course it is, James.'

His eyes bored into hers. 'You didn't go somewhere else on the way to Tim's, by any chance?'

'I went to a couple of places. I collected my things from the flat, and then I took my suit to the cleaners and bought some food.'

'No visits to clinics?' he demanded.

'Clinics?' she repeated blankly, then stared at him, incensed, as the penny dropped. 'Oh, I see! Well, you're wrong. A termination was one possibility I never even considered. I'm hardly likely to get rid of the only blood relative I might ever possess!'

He exhaled slowly, and rubbed a hand over his eyes. 'I had to ask, Harriet. My imagination went into overdrive when I couldn't find you.'

'I just needed breathing space, James,' she said, calming down. 'I knew Tim's place would be empty so I went there to think things over.'

He looked at her in silence for a moment, then crossed to the kitchen counter and leaned against it as though he needed support. 'And have you come to any conclusion?'

'Yes. Do you still want to marry me?'

'Yes, Harriet,' he said with weary emphasis, 'I still want to marry you. But something tells me you're about to make conditions.'

She nodded. 'You have to do something first.'

His eyes narrowed. 'What, exactly?'

'Take a DNA test. We'll have one, too,' She patted her midriff. 'That way you'll never have to ask again if the child is yours. You'll know. One way or the other.'

'To hell with that,' said James, appalled. 'I know I hurt you, Harriet, and I regret it bitterly. But this is pure retaliation.' He seized her hands. 'Look me in the eye, Harriet, and tell me there's even a remote possibility that I'm not the father.' He nodded in triumph as her eyes fell. 'You know you can't.'

'I still want you to have the test,' she said stubbornly, pulling away. 'Otherwise no wedding. I'd rather bring my child up on my own.'

'Over my dead body!'

Harriet shrugged and picked up her bag. 'I'm going back to the flat. You need time to think it over. Call me when you've decided.'

'I've already done that, so I'd rather you stayed here so I can look after you.' He took the bag from her, looking every year of his age for once. 'When I made a promise to your grandmother to look out for you I didn't know what I was letting myself in for. Nor that I would fall so hopelessly in love with you that I'd do any damn thing you wanted.' He shrugged wearily. 'You win, Harriet. I'll take the test.'

'This isn't a contest, James, it's not a case of winning,' she said, her voice purposely acid to disguise threatening tears.

'No. In my case it's losing.' He put the bag down and took hold of her by the shoulders. 'But remember this. You're the one insisting on the test, not me.'

'You're afraid of the result?'

'God grant me patience,' he said bitterly, his eyes locked with hers. 'I *know* the result. And so do you. But if that's what it takes to get you to marry me, I'll do it.'

'Thank you. Thank you for the furniture, too,' she added belatedly.

'Not at all,' said James with formality, and took her bag into the newly furnished spare room. 'There. It's all yours, Harriet. Put your feet up, read, watch television, or anything you like, then later perhaps you'll join me out here for dinner.'

She nodded, feeling suddenly forlorn. 'Do you want me to cook?'

'No. I'll send out for something. You need to rest. On Monday,' he said on his way to the door, 'you can serve notice that you're vacating the flat, ready to move in here next weekend.'

'James,' she said urgently.

He turned. 'Yes?'

'I'm sorry I worried you.'

His eyes softened a little. 'Next time you go walkabout leave a note, please.'

Once James closed the door behind him Harriet sat down

in her new, supremely comfortable chair. She looked at the furniture grouped so carefully with the television, the pile of new books on the bedside table. She had her own private sitting room, just as she'd asked for, but James obviously meant her to sleep in it as well. And after the dance she'd led him on, she could hardly complain.

The rest of the evening passed in a polite truce, with no physical contact between them other than James' kiss on Harriet's cheek before she retired to bed in her newly furnished room. After more of the same during Sunday, by early evening she was more than ready to go back to Clerkenwell.

'I'm London-based this week,' James informed her when they arrived at her flat.

She eyed him warily as she switched on lights. 'Will I see you before next weekend?'

'Do you want to?'

'If I don't want to, there's not much point in moving in with you,' she said tartly.

'Do you want to see me?' he repeated very deliberately.

'Not if it means a repeat of this weekend.'

'In that case maybe we should give each other some breathing space this week. But I'll be here first thing on Saturday morning. Until then take great care of yourself, please.' James took her in his arms and, for the first time since her life-altering announcement, kissed her very thoroughly before he let her go. 'Goodnight, Harriet. Sleep well.'

CHAPTER ELEVEN

DIDO PARKER, for all her candyfloss exterior, was the one person in the world Harriet knew she could trust with her momentous news. Not Tim this time, she thought with regret. This was one piece of news he'd have to learn from James.

'So that's why you fainted,' said Dido, once she'd recovered from the shock. 'I thought people only did that in films.'

'Me, too.'

'How do you feel about it? The baby, I mean.'

'Astonished, mainly.'

'Morning sickness yet?'

'The one time I've been sick was when I gave James the glad tidings.'

'How did he take it?'

'He asked if the baby was his, then held my head when I threw up in his kitchen sink.'

Dido shuddered. 'How *hideous*! Is that why you ran off to hide in Tim's house?'

Harriet nodded wryly. 'I was so hurt and angry I wanted him to suffer for that one split second of doubt.'

'James suffered all right! He was in a terrible state when he rang me. So was I,' added Dido with feeling.

'Sorry about that. I needed time on my own to think over James' proposal.'

'So he wants you to marry him then. Are you going to?'

'Of course I am.' Harriet smiled wistfully. 'He's the love

of my life, Dido—has been since I was thirteen years old, if we're counting. Otherwise I wouldn't dream of marrying him, baby or no baby.'

At the weekend James drove round to Clerkenwell to collect Harriet's belongings. He'd offered to hire a van for the purpose, but she'd assured him it was unnecessary.

'I can see why,' he said, surprised, when she let him in. 'Is this really everything?'

'I had to be ruthless when I moved in here. You see before you the sum total of my worldly possessions, other than the things you're storing for me.' Harriet smiled. 'Radio, books and CDs in the boxes, clothes in the cases, and the plant pot you gave me. That's it.'

When they got to the apartment James took her suitcases straight to his bedroom. 'I've cleared a space for you,' he said, sliding back one of his wardrobe doors. 'Your books can go downstairs in the office.'

After a week of little conversation with James other than a brief nightly phone call to inquire about her health, Harriet was relieved that the question of where to put her belongings had been answered before she'd asked it. 'I'm meeting Dido for lunch, by the way,' she said as she unpacked her clothes. 'We're going shopping for wedding gear. Tim's wedding,' she added awkwardly.

James leaned in the doorway. 'You'll need something for ours, too.'

'The same one will do for both, surely?' She turned to smile at him. 'It's pointless to buy things that won't fit me for long.'

'You only get married once—'

'Not always, James.'

The tawny eyes locked with hers. 'I intend to make very sure it's only once for you, Harriet.' He took out his wallet. 'You'll need some money.'

She shook her head. 'I'll pay for my own dress, James. Save your money for later. Babies cost a lot.'

'Have you told Tim about ours yet?'

'No, only Dido. Tim gave me such a telling off for worrying you—and him—last week, I left you to break the news.'

'In that case we'd better break it right away! I'll ask him round this evening. Or are you spending that with Dido, too?'

'No, I'm not.' She looked at him uncertainly. 'I'd assumed I'd spend it here with you.'

His eyes softened. 'So had I. Tim can share the meal I had ready for our lunch.'

'Sorry about that, James.' Harriet zipped up the last empty case and turned to face him. 'Your phone calls were so brief I never managed to tell you I was meeting Dido today.'

'It doesn't matter. I arranged about the test, by the way,' he added casually.

'Oh, right. Thank you,' she said, flushing.

'So now that's out of the way we can discuss the wedding.'

'Hold on,' said Harriet. 'We need test results before thinking about a wedding.'

He shook his head decisively. 'No, we don't, Harriet. All I need is a straight answer. Do you love me?'

'Yes,' she said simply.

He took her in his arms and kissed her victoriously. 'Then nothing else matters, test results least of all. Let's get married next Saturday. I'll make the arrangements while you're out.'

'As soon as that!' She stared at him in astonishment. 'James, are you serious?'

'Never more so. What point is there in waiting? You're

already here in my home and my life—and my heart,' he added, in a tone that finally settled the matter for Harriet.

'In that case, why not?' She smiled at him radiantly. 'Saturday it is.'

When Harriet got back from the shopping expedition James looked so worried she felt deeply contrite as he relieved her of a large hatbox and numerous smart carrier bags.

'Thank God,' he said fervently. 'I've been pacing the floor for the past half-hour. Why did you stay out so long? You look exhausted.'

'I am.' She kicked off her shoes with a groan and limped to a sofa. 'I may never go shopping again—at least, not with Dido. I didn't mean to worry you, James. I just lost track of the time.'

His eyes softened. 'What would you like to drink?'

'Water, please. Dido Parker, she I used to call friend, dragged me through every floor of Harvey Nichols on what must surely be the hottest day of the year!' She accepted a tall glass of mineral water and gulped it down thirstily.

James joined her on the sofa. 'Did you find what you wanted?'

'Yes.' She pushed her hair back from her damp forehead, and smiled at him. 'I found the perfect dress for the wedding, but I'm definitely wearing it to Tim's, too. And before you start lecturing, I ran out of energy, not money.'

'I suppose I'm not allowed to see this perfect dress until the day itself?'

'You bet. It's not a real wedding dress, by the way. You needn't wear a morning suit.'

'I'm going to just the same.' He smiled smugly. 'I look rather good in mine.'

She grinned. 'I bet you do. Talking of weddings, did you manage to get everything sorted for next week?'

'All arranged. The ceremony is at four next Saturday at

the church in Upcote, with a reception afterwards at Edenhurst,' he announced, his lips twitching as she stared at him, astounded. 'The only thing left to do is the licence.'

'Upcote?' she said faintly.

He shrugged. 'It seemed the obvious choice, for both of us. Your grandmother would certainly approve. I took it for granted you would, too, Harriet.'

'I do, I do. It's a lovely surprise, James,' she assured him. 'I'd assumed we'd just make for the nearest register office here in London.'

'I did that last time with well-known results.' James took her hand in his. 'Because I was the innocent party in the divorce the vicar's agreed to perform the ceremony. So I can make my vows to you, Harriet, in the sight of God as well as man.'

Deeply moved, she curled her fingers round his. 'James.'

He moved closer. 'What is it?'

'Now that we're actually getting married on Saturday— something I can't quite take in yet—can we go back to the way things were?'

He met her eyes squarely. 'Am I forgiven, then?'

'Yes,' she said soberly. 'Otherwise I wouldn't have gone shopping for a wedding dress. I hope you like the one I chose. It's a bit different from the normal things I buy. It wasn't on sale, for one thing. It's a size bigger than usual, too.'

James gave her a leisurely top to toe scrutiny. 'I can't see any difference.'

'I've put on an inch or so already round here,' she said, tapping her chest.

He grinned. 'You can hardly expect me to look on that as a disadvantage!'

Harriet chuckled, and James nodded in approval. 'That's better. I haven't heard you laugh much lately.'

'Sorry.' She patted her stomach. 'She's to blame.'

'It could be a he.'

'True. Would you prefer a boy, James?'

His grasp tightened for a moment as he helped her to her feet. 'All I ask is a healthy baby, Harriet, who gives its mother as little trouble as possible when it arrives.'

'Amen to that,' she said with feeling. 'I'd better hang my wedding finery away in my little retreat. And no peeking,' she added, smiling up at him.

'I wouldn't dream of it. I shall wait to be dazzled on the day. I'll carry the bags, and then leave you to it. Tim's coming at eight, so collect whatever you're wearing tonight, and then lie in the bath for a while, or better still, have a nap.'

'I think I will, but I'll be out in time to help with the meal,' she said, yawning widely as she trailed behind with her hatbox.

'There's nothing for you to do,' James assured her as he laid the bags down. 'It's just a selection of cold cuts and salads from my favourite food hall.' He grinned suddenly. 'If it isn't filling enough for Tim he can buy some fish and chips on his way home.'

When Harriet emerged from the spare room later in the terracotta dress, she was touched to see James had gone to some trouble to make the table look festive with champagne flutes and candles.

'How lovely,' she commented as he came out of the main bedroom.

'So are you,' said James. 'I like that dress.'

'Which is why I wore it,' she told him.

The tawny eyes lit with a heat she knew of old, but as James started towards her the bell rang and he smiled wryly, and went off to let his brother in.

'Sorry I'm late, folks,' said Tim, and gave Harriet a hug and kiss before standing back to look at her. 'Are you feeling better? No more faints? What have I said?' he added as she looked daggers at him.

'Faints in the plural?' demanded James.

'Oh, God,' groaned Tim. 'You didn't know?'

'About the one I witnessed, yes. Have there been more, Harriet, apart from the one when I went away?'

She nodded apologetically. 'When I had supper with Tim and Dido.'

'Scared the hell out of us,' said Tim, and raised his eyebrows as he saw the table. 'Hey, it's a special occasion! I should have worn my party dress.'

'Keep it for the wedding,' said his brother casually.

'No fear. I've got a really great suit for that,' said Tim with satisfaction. 'Francesca chose it.'

'Our wedding, not yours,' said James, removing the cork from a bottle of champagne.

Tim looked from his brother's face to Harriet's, then gave a whoop of triumph as he hugged the breath out of her then clapped James on the back. 'That's fantastic news! But you told me you were just moving in together, Harry.'

'We decided to tie the knot more permanently,' said James.

'Congratulations. When are you tying it?'

'Next Saturday,' Harriet informed him.

'*What?*' Tim sat down with a thump on one of the chairs at the table. 'This is all a bit sudden. You said you didn't want to get married last time the subject came up, Harry.'

'I changed my mind.'

'I changed it for her,' said James. 'We're having a baby.'

Tim stared at him, stunned, as he took a glass of champagne.

'Aren't you going to congratulate us, Uncle?' said Harriet, laughing.

'Lord, yes, it's marvellous news.' He raised his glass. 'Your very good health, both of you. Especially yours,

Harry. No wonder you fainted. I almost did myself just then. I can't wait to tell Francesca.'

'Tell her now,' said James, to his brother's delight. 'Ask her over for the wedding. You can both stay here with Harriet, if she's happy with that. I'll be in Upcote all week until the big day.' He smiled at a totally bemused Tim. 'I shall then take my bride to La Fattoria, and stay there until your own wedding, so if you want to show Francesca more of London you can use this place as a base.'

Tim leapt to his feet and hugged his brother, his eyes suspiciously damp. 'Thanks, James. I really appreciate that.'

'Go into the other room to ring Francesca,' said Harriet. 'Only don't fall over the furniture.'

Tim dashed off, exclaiming loudly over the new arrangement before sliding the spare room door closed behind him.

James handed a glass to Harriet. 'That obviously went well. He called me James for the first time.' He smiled wryly. 'I hope you don't mind sharing this place with Francesca for a night or two.'

'Of course not. Though I didn't realise I wouldn't see you for the entire week before the wedding.' She sighed. 'I'll miss you.'

He kissed her swiftly. 'I'll miss you a damn sight more. Let's drink a toast.'

She eyed the champagne warily. 'Should I be drinking this?'

'Just a sip or two for a toast.' James smiled into her eyes as he touched his glass to hers. 'To the three of us.'

'To the three of us,' echoed Harriet, her answering smile so blindingly happy James caught her in an embrace that lasted until Tim had to cough theatrically to interrupt them.

'Break it up, you two. I'm starving!'

At four o'clock to the minute the following Saturday, Harriet gave Dido a kiss in the doorway of St Mary's

Church, linked her arm through Tim's and, to the triumphant strains of Mendelssohn on the newly restored organ, walked down the aisle towards James, who looked so spectacularly handsome in his formal wedding clothes that after no sight of him for a week Harriet wanted to throw herself into his arms there and then. Instead she handed her posy of white roses to Dido and returned James' smile radiantly as he took her hand in his. Her dress, in double layers of pale pink chiffon printed with trailing white roses, coupled with a huge white straw hat, were both of them so foreign to her usual taste she'd been worried all week that she'd made a big mistake. But the look in James' eyes made it clear he thought she looked ravishing and she relaxed as Reverend Faraday, the vicar who'd known her since she was thirteen, began the words of the marriage service. When James received the ring from Nick Mayhew he looked down into Harriet's eyes as he put it on her finger, the conviction in his voice audible to everyone in the church as he made the vows that accompanied it. But when she slid a matching ring on his hand as she made the corresponding vows only Harriet heard his sharp intake of breath.

In the vestry, later, amongst all the kissing and congratulations James said in an undertone, 'The ring was a surprise. Thank you, Mrs Devereux.'

'I took a chance that you'd like it, Mr Devereux,' she whispered.

'I do. Enormously. I've never had one before.'

'I know. I did some research.'

When she took James' arm to walk down the aisle through a surprisingly crowded church Harriet smiled warmly on the familiar faces who'd come to wish her well, and laughed in delight when a silver horseshoe was thrust at her by a small person held aloft in his father's arms near the door.

'Robert!' exclaimed Harriet. 'Thank you.' She blew the little boy a kiss, and a smartly dressed Stacy grinned happily at her as she restored a rather chewed cuddly lion to her son.

Outside in the sunshine the bride and groom endured the usual photo shoot before escaping in a cloud of confetti to the car waiting to take them on the short journey to Edenhurst, where they received congratulations from the assembled staff before James finally managed to get his bride to himself for a moment before the guests arrived.

'You look so beautiful I'm almost afraid to spoil your perfection,' he said softly, taking her in his arms. 'I love you, Harriet.'

'I love you, too.' She raised her face for a kiss that was all too brief before the others began to arrive in the flower-filled dining room reserved for the purpose on this special day.

Tim rushed in first, swept Harriet into his arms, and hugged the life out of her before apologising to them both in an anguished undertone. 'Sorry! I forgot.'

'Baby and I don't mind hugging,' she whispered, and slid a look at James as Tim wrung his hand. 'In fact we like it.'

Her new husband grinned at her as Francesca kissed them both and wished them great happiness. 'You are a lucky man this time, James.'

He nodded in heartfelt agreement. 'The luckiest man in the world, Francesca.'

'I'm jolly glad this waterproof mascara's living up to its promises,' sniffed Dido as she kissed Harriet. 'You look utterly glorious today, sort of glowing.'

'It's a bride thing,' said Harriet as she hugged her friend. Then she held out her hand to Giles Kemble, accepted his kiss, introduced him to James, and passed him on to Dido, whose tears dried like magic when Giles acquired two glasses of champagne from a passing waiter and led her across the room.

'Brilliant idea to invite your boss,' murmured James, watching.

'In more ways than one,' Harriet said with satisfaction, and then turned with a smile as the Mayhews arrived to bestow congratulations, plus an invitation to the Cotswolds for a family weekend in the country when the newlyweds returned from honeymoon.

Because both bride and groom were short of relatives, the guest list was composed of colleagues and friends accompanied by partners of various kinds, and it was a congenial little crowd who enjoyed the excellent meal and the entertaining speeches. It was late in the evening by the time the tables were cleared and a trio began to play the kind of standards it was possible to dance to cheek to cheek. Amid cheers James led his now hatless bride onto the limited floor space.

'I asked for this type of music,' he murmured, 'so I could hold you in my arms at the earliest possible moment after the wedding.'

'How clever of you,' she said, impressed. 'You dance well, too.'

'So do you. Rather surprising for one of your tender years.'

Harriet chuckled as the music changed tempo and other couples joined them on the floor. 'A woman must always be able to surprise her man. I read it in a magazine.'

She was allowed only the first dance with her husband. After that Harriet danced with Tim, then one man after another until James led her to her seat at last, gave her a glass of water and told her she looked tired.

'At the risk of being misunderstood,' he said in her ear, 'I think I should get you to bed soon. You look tired.'

The moment James said it Harriet realised she was very tired indeed.

'I am,' she said apologetically. 'But I don't want this lovely day to end.'

He smiled with tenderness that turned her heart over. 'Nevertheless, bride, I'm going to carry you off. No one will be surprised that I want to.'

James stood up, signalled to the leader of the trio, and then tapped on his glass when the music stopped. 'My wife and I,' he began, and grinned at the catcalls and applause, 'thank you all for coming to share in our happy day. Please stay as long as you like to enjoy the party, but we have a journey to make tomorrow and my bride is beginning to show signs of fatigue, so—'

'Come off it, Jed,' hooted someone. 'You just want to take her off to bed.'

'You're absolutely right, I do,' said James, unruffled, and held out his hand to Harriet.

She smiled on the assembled company as she got up. 'Goodnight, everyone. Enjoy the rest of the party.'

After kisses from Tim, Francesca and Dido, James took Harriet's arm and led her from the room to the strains of the Wagner Wedding March from the trio, but once in the hall he said goodnight to the porter, and took his yawning bride out into the starry night instead of up the main staircase as she'd expected.

'Where are we going?' she asked, surprised.

'Home to my place.'

It seemed a very long way across the cobbled courtyard to the stable flat. By the time they reached it Harriet was too tired to do more than give a cursory glance at her surroundings. But as James swung her feet up on a very comfortable sofa she smiled as she spotted her grandmother's cabinet and lacquer screen.

'Just like home,' she said drowsily.

'Want some tea?' he asked, undoing his tie.

'More than anything in the world at this moment,' she assured him.

But when James Devereux got back with the tray Stacy had put ready for them, his bride was fast asleep. Smiling wryly, he picked Harriet up and carried her into the bedroom. With infinite care he undid the fragile dress and slid it off, decided she could sleep in what little she had on underneath, and pulled the covers over her, then kissed her cheek before going into the other room to drink tea. He grinned as he filled the delicate cup Stacy had considered appropriate to the occasion. This wasn't exactly standard procedure for a wedding night. But now Harriet was safely married to him he was a happy man just the same.

It was late on the following day, under a sky too bright with stars to be totally dark, when James drove through the archway into the courtyard of La Fattoria, where welcoming lights shone from the windows, but otherwise all was quiet.

'After spending time with Francesca and Tim, plus Dido the night before the wedding, I thought you might fancy a little peace and quiet,' he said as he helped Harriet out of the car. 'I told the Capellinis they could wait a day or two before they met my bride.'

'Thank you for that, James. Peace and quiet sounds very appealing. I like Francesca very much, but I had to keep reassuring her that I was happy about her marriage to Tim,' Harriet told him ruefully. 'It got a bit wearing.'

'I'm more interested in whether you're happy about your marriage to me,' said James, and picked her up. 'Time-honoured custom,' he reminded her as he carried her over the threshold.

Harriet smiled with pleasure as he put her down in the cool, familiar kitchen. 'I love this place, James.'

'So do I.' He went out to fetch their luggage, refusing her offers of help. 'You had an exhausting day yesterday,' he reminded her when he came back.

'But a happy, lovely day. I like your friends, the Mayhews. Did I tell you Lydia asked us for a weekend in the Cotswolds when we get back?'

'Good, but don't think about going back right now.' James took her hands. 'Let's enjoy our time here first.'

'Since this is the only honeymoon I'll ever have I'm in full agreement.'

'You do look on it as a honeymoon, then?'

Harriet looked up at his tense face in surprise. 'Of course I do. After such a beautiful wedding day yesterday, what else could it be?'

'Just a holiday, maybe?' He looked at her very directly. 'I rushed you to the altar so fast you might well need breathing space. To get used to being my wife,' he added.

Harriet looked at him in silence for a moment. They hadn't shared a bed since James had learned about the baby. After her shopping expedition with Dido their reconciliation had been sweet, but it had been followed by the celebration dinner with Tim, after which she'd been so tired that James had insisted on sleeping in the spare room before he left next day for Upcote to make the wedding arrangements. And when she woke this morning, surprised to find she was in her grandmother's brass bed, Harriet had found to her dismay that her wedding night had come and gone, and her smiling husband stood fully dressed at her bedside, bearing a breakfast tray.

'I can see why you might think that way,' she said at last.

'What do you mean?'

'I've been a pretty unsatisfactory bride so far!'

'Not to me,' he assured her.

Deciding that it was time to make things clear Harriet chose her words with care. 'You made our wedding day as perfect for me as any woman could wish for, James. And today we've flown here first class—which *was* a first for me—and then we had a delicious meal in that little trattoria tonight on the way to this beautiful, peaceful house.' She reached up and kissed him lightly. 'If this isn't a honeymoon, James Edward Devereux, what is?'

She could hardly make it plainer than that, Harriet thought as she followed James up the winding stairs to the tower room, where a vase of pink and white roses stood on the chest, filling the air with their perfume.

'I've left the rest of the luggage downstairs,' he said, putting her overnight bag on the settle. 'Let's leave the unpacking until tomorrow.'

'Amen to that,' she said with a sigh, and with loving care laid her wedding hat on the top shelf of the armoire.

'By the way, I've got something for you, Harriet,' said James, taking an envelope from his jacket pocket. 'Stacy handed it to me first thing before you got up.'

She felt a little thrill when she saw the envelope was addressed to Mr & Mrs Devereux, and took out a card embellished with hearts and horseshoes, and a photograph of a beaming toddler.

'Congratulations and best wishes from Stacy and Greg, and a big kiss from Robert.'

'How lovely,' said Harriet, delighted. 'We must put it with the others. Thank Stacy for me when you go down to Upcote.'

'Come with me and thank her yourself,' he suggested.

'I may well do that, now I've seen your flat. I love it, James.'

'I once asked you to dinner there,' he reminded her, 'but you turned me down.'

She felt her colour rise. 'I was afraid.'

His eyebrows shot together. 'Of *me*?'

'Not exactly. But I was still pretending to be Tim's bride-to-be at the time, remember. The fiction was a bit difficult to keep up when one touch of your hand was enough to turn me to jelly. It still is,' she added, looking him in the eye.

James let out a deep sigh and took her in his arms, leaning his forehead against hers. 'Thank God for that.' He kissed her fleetingly and let her go. 'I'd better leave you to your bath. Shall I make you some tea?'

'No, thanks. I'm off tea, big time. I'd like a big bottle of mineral water, please.'

'Now?'

Harriet gave him a look designed to make her expectations crystal clear. 'Bring it when you come to bed.'

She spent such a short time in the bath it seemed ages before James came back. She smiled at him from her perch on the settle by the window, hoping he approved of the brief apricot silk nightgown she'd chosen alone one day in her lunch hour.

'You were a long time, James.'

He smiled as his eyes travelled over her with appreciation. 'You normally like to wallow in the bath so I had a shower while I was waiting,' he said, and put a tray with glasses and bottles down beside the roses. He joined her on the settle and took her hand in his. 'You looked utterly beautiful as you came down the aisle to me yesterday, Harriet.'

'Brides are required to,' she informed him. 'It goes with the job description. Thank you for my bouquet, the roses were perfect. Did you choose white as a safe bet?'

'Not at all. I consulted Dido.'

'Did you arrange for these, too?'

He nodded. 'But I think they should go somewhere else tonight. The scent is overpowering. I'll put them in the other room.'

While James was gone Harriet drank some water, and sat gazing out into the starlit darkness as she thought over her glorious wedding day. She was glad James had liked her choice of bridal finery. If she'd looked beautiful for him it had been worth every penny of the outrageous price she'd paid for it all.

When he returned she got up, knowing that before she could get on with being married to James Devereux she had to give him the information that was the only cloud on her horizon.

'I've got a confession to make, James,' she said baldly.

He eyed her in alarm. 'There's nothing wrong with the baby?'

'No. We're both fine. It's just that, well, I didn't have a DNA test,' she finished in a rush. 'I was going to tell you not to have one, either, but you were too quick for me. You'd already had one.'

James let out a deep breath. 'Is that your big confession?'

She nodded dumbly.

'I've got an even bigger one.' He met her eyes squarely. 'I didn't have the test, either. I just said I did to make sure you turned up yesterday.'

'You *lied*?'

'With the best of intentions,' he said, unrepentant, and tipped her face up to his. 'You're mine, both of you, and if I had to lie to make sure you married me I don't care a damn.' He kissed her fiercely, and she kissed him back.

'There's something else I haven't told you,' she informed him, smiling at him radiantly.

'It can't be bad if you're smiling,' he said warily.

'Our baby's birthday will be nine months from the night you first made love to me in that bed over there.'

'I was sure of that already.' James picked her up and carried her over to the bed. 'I want to make love to you in it again right now,' he informed her.

'I should think so,' said Harriet, kissing his throat. 'After all, this is our honeymoon, Mr Devereux.'

'Thank God for that, too,' he said as he set her on her feet. 'At one point I had serious doubts that I'd get you to marry me, darling, baby or not.'

'I married you because I love you, James, it's as simple as that.' She reached up to kiss him. 'Besides, I've always known you were the father of my baby.'

'So have I. But I was afraid, in that first, blood-curdling moment, that you were going to tell me someone else was the father, so I asked the question that could have ruined our lives. My life, anyway.'

'Mine, too.' She lifted her face to receive his kiss, and James touched a hand to the silk covering her breasts, and made a relishing sound as he traced the new fullness with a not quite steady hand.

'I've been too long without you. Come to bed,' he urged, shrugging off his dressing gown. 'This thing you're wearing is very pretty, my darling. Take it off.'

Harriet obliged, laughing, and flowed into his arms, relishing the feel of skin against skin as James began kissing her.

'You said this is the only honeymoon you'll ever have,' he whispered. 'So we'll savour it together, my darling.' He drew her down with him to kiss her with slow, erotic kisses that were an end in themselves instead of merely the overture to what would come next. Harriet gave herself up to the joy of his skilled, lingering mouth, shivering in delight as his hands slid over her skin to shape her breasts and hips, and move tenderly over the gentle swell between them.

'I love you, Mrs Devereux,' he whispered.

'I love you, too, Mr Devereux.'

He kissed her with sudden urgency. 'Show me how much.'

Harriet slid a caressing hand over his shoulders and down his back, glorying in the tightening of his muscles under her questing fingers. She kissed him, open-mouthed, caressing his tongue with hers, and then slid her mouth down his taut throat and caught his flat nipples between her teasing teeth before moving her lips down his flat stomach and James breathed in sharply and pulled her beneath him, kissing her with a ravening demand that thrilled Harriet to the core. She writhed in hot, delectable anguish as his seeking fingers found the proof of how much she wanted him, and pleaded with him in such husky desperation James lifted her hips and fused his body to hers. At first, in deference to the baby, he made love to her with all the care and restraint at his command, but soon his bride demonstrated a fiery urgency he was powerless to resist, and they surged together in such harmony they reached the final pinnacle of sensation in unison.

They lay locked in each other's arms afterwards, unwilling to separate. It was a long time before James raised his head to look into Harriet's eyes.

'You know what, Mrs Devereux? I've just discovered an incontrovertible truth. Marriage is not the cure for love, after all.'

Harriet smiled lovingly, and stroked the damp hair back from her husband's forehead. 'We haven't been married long enough to know, surely!'

'You're missing the point.' James kissed her stroking hand. 'I meant that the love I feel for you is with me for life. There is no cure.'

'You mean you're stuck with it.'

He laughed. 'Yes, my unromantic darling, I'm stuck with it.'

'So am I.' She met his eyes with a look so blazingly happy it took his breath away. 'For as long as we both shall live.'

Your opinion is important to us!

Please take a few moments to share your thoughts with us about Mills & Boon® and Silhouette® books. Your comments will ensure that we continue to deliver books you love to read.

To thank you for your input, everyone who replies will be entered into a prize draw to win a year's supply of their favourite series books*.

1. There are several different series under the Mills & Boon and Silhouette brands. Please tick the box that most accurately represents your reading habit for each series.

Series	Currently Read (have read within last three months)	Used to Read (but do not read currently)	Do Not Read
Mills & Boon			
Modern Romance™	❑	❑	❑
Sensual Romance™	❑	❑	❑
Blaze™	❑	❑	❑
Tender Romance™	❑	❑	❑
Medical Romance™	❑	❑	❑
Historical Romance™	❑	❑	❑
Silhouette			
Special Edition™	❑	❑	❑
Superromance™	❑	❑	❑
Desire™	❑	❑	❑
Sensation™	❑	❑	❑
Intrigue™	❑	❑	❑

2. Where did you buy this book?

From a supermarket ❑ Through our Reader Service™ ❑
From a bookshop ❑ If so please give us your Club Subscription no.
On the Internet ❑
Other _____ _____/_____

3. Please indicate by number which were the 3 most important factors that made you buy this book. (1 = most important).

The picture on the cover ___ I enjoy this series ___
The author ___ The price ___
The title ___ I borrowed/was given this book ___
The description on the back cover ___ Part of a mini-series ___

Other _____

4. How many Mills & Boon and /or Silhouette books do you buy at one time?

I buy ___ books at one time ❑
I rarely buy a book (less than once a year) ❑

5. How often do you shop for any Mills & Boon and/or Silhouette books?

One or more times a month ❑ A few times per year ❑
Once every 2-3 months ❑ Never ❑

6. How long have you been reading Mills & Boon® and/or Silhouette®?
_____ years

7. What other types of book do you enjoy reading?

Family sagas eg. Maeve Binchy ☐
Classics eg. Jane Austen ☐
Historical sagas eg. Josephine Cox ☐
Crime/Thrillers eg. John Grisham ☐
Romance eg. Danielle Steel ☐
Science Fiction/Fantasy eg. JRR Tolkien ☐
Contemporary Women's fiction eg. Marian Keyes ☐

8. Do you agree with the following statements about Mills & Boon? Please tick the appropriate boxes.

	Strongly agree	Tend to agree	Neither agree nor disagree	Tend to disagree	Strongly disagree
Mills & Boon offers great value for money.	☐	☐	☐	☐	☐
With Mills & Boon I can always find the right type of story to suit my mood.	☐	☐	☐	☐	☐
I read Mills & Boon books because they offer me an entertaining escape from everyday life.	☐	☐	☐	☐	☐
Mills & Boon stories have improved or stayed the same standard over the time I have been reading them.	☐	☐	☐	☐	☐

9. Which age bracket do you belong to? Your answers will remain confidential.

☐ 16-24   ☐ 25-34   ☐ 35-49   ☐ 50-64   ☐ 65+

THANK YOU for taking the time to tell us what you think! If you would like to be entered into the **FREE prize draw** to win a year's supply of your favourite series books, please enter your name and address below.

Name: _____

Address: _____

_____

Post Code: _____ Tel: _____

Please send your completed questionnaire to the address below:

READER SURVEY, PO Box 676, Richmond, Surrey, TW9 1WU.

* Prize is equivalent to 4 books a month, for twelve months, for your chosen series. No purchase necessary. To obtain a questionnaire and entry form, please write to the address above. Closing date 31st December 2004. Draw date no later than 15th January 2005. Full set of rules available upon request. Open to all residents of the UK and Eire, aged 18 years and over.

As a result of this application, you may receive offers from Harlequin Mills & Boon Ltd. If you do not wish to share in this opportunity please write to the data manager at the address shown above. ® and ™ are trademarks owned and used by the owner and/or its licensee.

MILLS & BOON®

0904/01b

Live the emotion

Modern
romance™

SURRENDER TO MARRIAGE *by Sandra Field*

Billionaire Jake Reilly has returned to claim Shaine O'Sullivan
– and he's not about to take no for an answer. But how can
she live the life of glamour and riches to which Jake has
grown accustomed? Especially when she's concealing from
him the biggest secret of all...

IN McGILLIVRAY'S BED *by Anne McAllister*

Sydney St John has to escape her deeply unattractive business
partner, who's demanding that she marry him. Hugh
McGillivray has the solution: by pretending to be *his* wife. Fine
in theory – but it means they'll have to act married, do the
things that married couples do...like share a bed!

A BRIDE FOR HIS CONVENIENCE *by Lindsay Armstrong*

Virginal Caiti had given millionaire Rob Leicester everything –
and had been overjoyed when they wed. But her joy turned
to shame when she discovered Rob had married her purely
for convenience, so she left him. But Rob was now ready to
claim her – this time as his wife for real!

PREGNANCY OF PASSION *by Lucy Monroe*

Elisa trusted Salvatore di Vitale about as far as she could
throw him – and as the Sicilian security expert was over six
feet of muscle, that wasn't very far! He had told her he had
come to protect her. But if their close proximity led to
passion he wouldn't exactly be complaining...

Don't miss out...

On sale 1st October 2004

*Available at most branches of WHSmith, Tesco, ASDA, Martins,
Borders, Eason, Sainsbury's and all good paperback bookshops.*

Lynne
Graham

International Playboys

*An Insatiable
Passion*

FREE!

4 Books
and a surprise gift!

We would like to take this opportunity to thank you for reading this Mills & Boon® book by offering you the chance to take FOUR more specially selected titles from the Modern Romance™ series absolutely FREE! We're also making this offer to introduce you to the benefits of the Reader Service™—

- ★ FREE home delivery
- ★ FREE gifts and competitions
- ★ FREE monthly Newsletter
- ★ Exclusive Reader Service offers
- ★ Books available before they're in the shops

Accepting these FREE books and gift places you under no obligation to buy, you may cancel at any time, even after receiving your free shipment. Simply complete your details below and return the entire page to the address below. You don't even need a stamp!

YES! Please send me 4 free Modern Romance books and a surprise gift. I understand that unless you hear from me, I will receive 6 superb new titles every month for just £2.69 each, postage and packing free. I am under no obligation to purchase any books and may cancel my subscription at any time. The free books and gift will be mine to keep in any case.

P4ZEF

Ms/Mrs/Miss/Mr ....Initials ....
BLOCK CAPITALS PLEASE

Surname ....

Address ....

....

....Postcode ....

Send this whole page to:
UK: FREEPOST CN8I, Croydon, CR9 3WZ